Bright Shining Moment

Bright Shining Moment

Deb Loughead

Second Story Press

Library and Archives Canada Cataloguing in Publication

Loughead, Deb, 1955-, author
Bright shining moment / Deb Loughead.

Issued in print and electronic formats.
ISBN 978-1-77260-068-1 (softcover).--ISBN 978-1-77260-072-8 (HTML)

I. Title.

PS8573.O8633B54 2018   jC813'.54   C2018-900422-3
                                                 C2018-900423-1

ISBN: 978-1-77260-068-1 (softcover)
ISBN 978-1-77260-072-8 (e-book)

Printed and bound in Canada

Text © Deb Loughead
Cover image © François Thisdale
Edited by Heather Camlot
Designed by Ellie Sipila

Second Story Press gratefully acknowledges the support of the Ontario Arts Council
and the Canada Council for the Arts for our publishing program. We acknowledge the
financial support of the Government of Canada through the Canada Book Fund.

Published by
SECOND STORY PRESS
20 Maud Street, Suite 401
Toronto, ON M5V 2M5
www.secondstorypress.ca

For my mom, Laurie Symsyk (née Laurette Saumur), whose evocative Ottawa stories, shared over a lifetime, continue to enrich my imagination. Thanks so much for everything you've given me.

1

Chewing Gum

On Wednesday afternoon, when our teacher asks who can bring used chewing gum to school tomorrow, lots of hands go up in the air. I know that I won't be able to help her, though.

Sister Madeleine needs our gum for sticking things on the blackboard and the wall. She says it works very well for that. But I don't have any chewing gum and don't know when I ever will. Except for now and then, when my friend Thérèse Beaudoin gives me a bit of hers that doesn't even have any taste left, I never get to have gum in my mouth. Once, when nobody was looking, I picked a piece off the sidewalk that was hardly chewed at all and still had some flavor left in it. That was heavenly.

I really wish I could have some gum to bring to school for Sister on Thursday. When I look around the classroom, some of my other classmates don't have their hands up. Instead, they stare at their desks, and I know why. Those girls are ashamed, just like I am. Their families have no money to buy gum, either.

Jeanine Bonenfant has her hand in the air, though. She never puts up her hand to answer questions the way I do because she never knows the answer. But when Sister asks if anyone can bring their chewing gum to school, she can finally raise her hand. She seems very proud right now and has a big wide smile, and Jeanine usually just scowls all day—when she isn't getting the strap. And when she gets it, she just half-smiles at the rest of us as she walks back to her desk. But she can bring used gum to school, and I know she's even poorer than we are. I also know a secret about her. I know why she has money for gum.

For the rest of the day, I'm mad. I can't believe Jeanine will have some used chewing gum to bring for Sister tomorrow and I won't. It isn't fair. My face gets red every time I look over at her, slouched there at the back of the class at her desk and not doing her work. When Sister asks her to write a word on the blackboard, she spells it wrong, then swears out loud, "*Maudit*," and gets the strap. Three smacks on each hand. I secretly rejoice. Ha! I might not have any gum, but at least I can spell. At least I always get As and red checkmarks. At least Sister never has a reason to get mad or yell at me. She even asks me to help her after school sometimes. And I never get the strap.

Today it's impossibly hard to hold on to my secret about Jeanine, especially when I'm jealous that she has gum to bring for Sister. And after school I can't hold it in any longer. It almost burns my tongue because I'm still so mad about the chewing gum that I don't have.

That's why I decide to tell my cousin Lucille, who lives across the road from us and has the same last name as we do. Our fathers never speak to each other because a long time ago my papa had a fight with his brother Pierre, who is Lucille's papa. When I ask *Maman* to explain, she says it's just too complicated for a child to understand. But I still like Lucille, even though she's only eleven—a year younger than I am, a year older than my sister, Yvette, and in Grade 5. Papa doesn't know that I walk home every day with Lucille, that I play with her at recess, and that she's my close chum.

Thérèse is walking home with us today too. She's taller than me, with blue eyes, black hair, and a pretty nose. She has a French father and an English mother, and she can speak English very well compared to me. Her father has a good job. He is a butcher. They have a very nice house a few streets away from ours and a garage with a car in it instead of a barn with horses, like we have. I never invite her to our house. Ours is very different from the other people's houses around here, and sometimes I feel ashamed about that.

But I know for sure that Jeanine steals money, and I can't hold on to this secret any longer. When I tell them, Lucille's eyes open wide and so does her mouth.

"And that's why she always has money for gum and candy and Sister's charity box," I say, enjoying the shock on her face.

"How do you know that, Aline?" she gasps.

"That's a secret too," I tell her.

I don't want to confess to her that I overheard the bread man, Monsieur Nadeau, telling my mother one day when I was home sick from school. I'm not sure how he found out, but somehow our bread man knows everything about everybody around here. He sees things that nobody else sees, and hears them too. Sometimes I think he knows everybody's secrets.

Monsieur Nadeau always stops and talks to Maman. That's how she finds out what's going on in our neighborhood, here in Paroisse Saint-François d'Assise. She says that sometimes he tells her things that she really doesn't want to know. Papa says that he tells too much that's none of his business, that he should just deliver his baked goods and leave his gossip in his bread wagon.

"I already knew that," Thérèse tells us with a sneaky grin. She loves to hear gossip, especially when it's bad. "Jeanine always steals from her mother's purse. And from her father's pockets when he's asleep."

"But why don't they ever catch her?" Lucille asks.

Thérèse snorts. "Because her papa is a big drunk. And her maman sleeps all day. You know sometimes she has bugs in her hair, and her brothers and sisters too. And they wear used clothes that are always dirty."

I feel my face turn red. I don't want to tell them that we've had bugs too, my sister and brothers and I. We had to sit at the table over a newspaper while Maman used a special comb to get the eggs out of our hair. Then she washed our hair with very hot water and stinky soap. And sometimes we wear used clothes too, but they're always clean.

"That's terrible," Lucille says. "She's breaking a commandment. She's in big trouble."

"I know. She's a sinner. Don't tell anyone, okay?" I beg them.

Thérèse says good-bye to us a few blocks from our street. I hope I can trust her with my secret. As we round the corner onto Hinchey Avenue, my cousin and I unlink our arms and walk on separate sides of the road. I don't want Maman to see me through the kitchen window walking with Lucille in case she mentions it to Papa, because that might make him unhappy with me. And I don't like it when that happens.

"How was your day at school, *ma belle*?" Maman asks when I walk through the door.

"*Très bonne*, Maman," I tell her, even though it wasn't even close to being very good.

The first thing I do on Thursday morning is let out a gasp. The wood floor is still freezing when I climb out of bed because the house hasn't warmed up yet after Papa filled the furnace with wood this morning. The second thing I do is toss a pillow at my younger sister, who was curled up tight under the quilt beside me all night.

"Get up, Yvette. It's time to get ready for school," I tell her. Yvette rolls over and moans, just like every morning.

"I don't want to go today." She starts to cough into her pillow again. Sometimes she wakes me up with her coughing.

"You never want to go." I tug on a pair of thick wool socks and shuffle out of the bedroom and into the bathroom to splash cold water on my face. As usual, I scowl in the mirror at my tangled mane of dark brown hair. I twist it atop my head, then frown as it drops around my shoulders like a rumpled veil.

I press on the bridge of my nose. The bump turns white for a second, then fills in again. Last night, once again, I fell asleep while pressing the end of my ugly nose upward, praying to Sainte-Thérèse for a miracle to make it stay that way, to make it look more like an "English" nose by morning. It's my someday dream. But once again, it hasn't come true. I make an ugly face at myself and hurry down to breakfast.

Maman is in her house dress, her hair in a loose bun already, stirring the porridge at the stove and frying potatoes and pork for Papa. She wears sturdy black shoes. She's not so tall, but she's thick and sturdy, just like her shoes. Papa is taller, but sturdy too, with a square, hard face, not roundish and soft like Maman's. Maman's lips curl up more than our father's do, and she has wrinkles around her eyes whenever she smiles. Papa doesn't smile as much as she does. He gets meat and potatoes for breakfast every morning because he has to work out in the cold. We get the same mushy, old porridge.

"Again?" I say, and Maman narrows her eyes at me.

"Can I have some sugar on it, *please*?" I ask. "Just a tiny bit."

"I need it for baking. You know that, so stop asking."

"There will be more rations during this war," Arthur says. Our older brother, with his white face, is reading the paper like he does every morning. He almost never plays outside. Maman says he thinks too much and needs some fresh air. "You'll see. First, it was sugar and coffee and tea. Next month, ration coupons for butter. There will be more to come next year."

"Maybe not," I tell my brother. "You don't know everything, Arthur."

"There will be. I know what's coming because I read about what's happening in the world. Not silly romance novels like you always read."

I make a face at him and stir my porridge. I don't know everything about the war the way Arthur does, and he always likes to brag about it too.

"The Dionnes eat this kind of oatmeal," Maman tells me.

I just shrug and scowl. That doesn't work anymore. The Dionne quintuplets are getting older, and so am I. I don't care so much now about what they eat or what toothpaste they brush their teeth with or what they do in their little playground with the fence around it that everyone in the world still goes to visit way up north in Callander, Ontario. I don't care if they're rich and get everything for free, either. They are like animals in a zoo. But lucky ones, that's for sure, with their nurses and all their new toys and their special colors and symbols so that people can tell them apart. I would want to be blue like Marie, but with a lollipop for my symbol, not a teddy bear.

Bernard is sitting at the table too, not paying attention to anything we're saying. Instead, our younger brother has his hands clasped in front of him, his eyes closed.

"You're praying again?" I ask Bernard. He doesn't answer me.

"He prays all the time," Arthur answers for him. "He wants to be a Christian Brother, like our teachers at school, remember?"

Maman looks at us over her shoulder. Her face turns into a frown.

"Where's Yvette?" she asks. "Why isn't she coming down yet?"

"I don't think she wants to go to school today," I tell Maman.

"She never wants to go to school," says Arthur, peering over the top of his paper.

"Maybe she's really one of the Bonenfant children, not a Sauriol like us. Maybe she should be in their family instead of ours." I grin at Arthur, and we both laugh.

"That's not funny. That's mean," our younger brother tells us.

"Oh, listen to *Frère* Bernard telling us when to laugh," Arthur says. "Give us your blessing this morning, Frère Bernard."

Bernard sticks out his tongue at us, and we laugh again—even Bernard this time.

"Go upstairs and get your sister, Aline." Maman stands with the wooden spoon in her hand, stabbing it toward the stairway. "Go and get her right now. She'll be late for a ride to school with Papa."

"Let her be late, Maman. It will do her good to get in trouble from the teacher. Maybe next time she won't stay in bed so long." I want to stay in the kitchen by the warm stove.

"*Vas-y*, Adéline." She points with the wooden spoon again. "Go!" Adéline is my real name even though most people call me Aline. When Maman uses my real name, I have to hurry.

I slip and slide in my wooly socks along the kitchen floor to the stairway as though I'm on skates and stamp up halfway to the landing.

"Yvette! *Dépêche-toi*! Hurry! We'll be late!"

The only sound that comes from our bedroom is a muffled moan.

"She won't come down, Maman," I tell her in the kitchen. "And she was coughing all night again too."

"Don't tell me poor Yvette is sick again." Maman clucks her tongue and her face sags with worry.

The two barn cats, a brown striped one and a black one, weave around her ankles at the back door, waiting to be let outside. Our mother lets them sleep indoors by the stove at night whenever it's freezing cold because she feels sorry for them. If they don't come when she calls "*minou, minou*" just before bed, she stomps across the snowy yard to the barn to get them. She carries them into the kitchen, one under each arm, then even gives them a few drops of milk. She smiles whenever she hears them purring because she knows they're warm and safe. They are like a part of the furniture in the kitchen, but they're not terribly friendly, so I hardly ever bother with them, except maybe for a pat or two in passing.

"It's her tonsils again." Maman bends to stroke each cat between the ears, then opens the back door for them before they start to scratch at the door frame. She shakes her head as she pulls the door shut. "Poor Yvette. Time to make *la soupe de malade.*"

Maman makes the special creamy soup with crushed tomatoes and milk for us whenever we're too sick to eat. We all love that soup, with crackers, but don't like being sick enough that our mother needs to make it for us.

La soupe de malade must mean Yvette is really sick.

2

Store-bought Hats

Out in the backyard, snowflakes float in the frozen air and clump on my eyelashes. Winter arrived in November this year. The horses stamp their huge hairy hooves and snort great plumes of steam. Their whiskers are already white with frost. Papa climbs aboard his old sled that he uses to deliver wood and fingers the reins.

"*Allons-y*, Aline," he calls to me. "Let's go!"

I climb slowly into the sled as my bundled-up brothers set off for École Saint-François-d'Assise, the boys' school a couple of blocks away on Stirling Avenue.

"Yvette is still in bed," I tell Papa. "She's going to get it from her teacher today—if Yvette ever shows up."

Papa steers the sled out of the yard. The clomping echoes in the winter air. Nobody ever rides around in sleds or wagons, except for the bread man, the milkman, and the iceman. And the rag-and-bone man. Yet we have both parked in our yard—a sled for the winter and a wagon for the rest of the time. And even worse, sometimes Papa takes my sister and me to school in the horrid old things, like he's doing today. Heads turn as we glide along the parish streets toward École Sacré-Coeur, where I'll be dropped off.

Children point and laugh. Someone I know throws a snowball that smashes against the side, spraying snow in my face: the biggest girl in my class, Jeanine Bonenfant. She has failed twice already, and she is always in trouble and seems to enjoy it. Papa stares straight ahead. I slide down into the hay, deeper and deeper until I'm almost entirely covered. I lie buried there until the sled shudders to a stop and I know we've reached my school. Now comes the hard part—to climb out without being noticed by the other students.

I quickly gather my books, slither over the back, and drop to the ground with a heavy thump. Then I brush the telltale straws of hay off my clothes and pick them out of my hair as the sled glides away.

The Grade 6 girls, wearing our uniform of black dresses with white collars, sit as still as statues at our desks as Sister Madeleine, with her rosary beads clacking, swishes up and down the aisles checking our homework. She has already collected the gum from everyone who could bring it. She walked around the classroom with a little bowl, and all the lucky girls who had some got to drop in their used gum. When she passed my desk, I didn't even look up. But I could feel my cheeks burning red, and I felt as if everyone in the class must be staring at me, Aline Sauriol, the girl who didn't bring chewed gum to school.

Sister Madeleine places a great red checkmark on my page of arithmetic. Perfect again. I beam up at her, but she ignores me, her narrow face set in a scowl, one eye on an empty desk that still awaits one of her students. Then, as Sister moves along the aisle, there's a racket from the back of the class, and everyone turns around to look. My friend Georgette Blondin, who sits behind me, snickers as she pokes me in the back. She has a nice house too, and such beautiful dolls, and sometimes I'm lucky because she invites me over to play.

Jeanine Bonenfant, the same girl who threw the snowball at our sled, has arrived, late as usual. The door crashes shut behind her. She drops her armload of books onto her desk and thumps down the aisle to the cloakroom in sloppy boots two sizes too big. She hangs her coat on the hook, slams that door, shuffles back up the aisle, and slumps into her chair. She sits there chewing a wad of gum and grinning. Sister Madeleine stands frozen in the middle of the classroom, her pencil in her hand, her nostrils flaring, spots of crimson glowing on her cheeks.

"Why are you late again today, Jeanine?" she asks.

"*Maudit*," we hear Jeanine mumble. And we can tell that Sister heard her too.

Slowly, Sister Madeleine drifts back to her desk like a huge black crow coming in for a landing and opens the drawer. Everyone in the classroom sits perfectly still, watching and waiting, not even daring to breathe. We all know what's coming next because the same thing happens almost every day.

"Jeanine. *Viens ici.*" Come here.

Jeanine sighs. She shambles to the front of the class and holds out her hands, palms facing up. Sister gives five hard smacks to each hand. I shiver just imagining how much it must sting. Jeanine smirks at her, then takes her gum out of her mouth, and drops it on Sister's desk. Sister gives her five more whacks. By now, her hands must be as tough as the soles of her rubber boots.

"Take off those boots and put them in the cloakroom," Sister tells her. "You know better than that by now."

"But I haven't got any stockings on today, Sister."

"Take them off anyway, please. The floors are already too wet. And try to walk where it's dry when you return to your desk."

Jeanine sighs again. She shuffles back to the cloakroom and kicks off her boots. Her feet are dirty. And they stink. Everyone wants to laugh, but no one dares. Not just for fear of making Sister even angrier, but because we all know Jeanine will ambush you on the way home from school if you laugh at her. Then she'll scrub your face with snow, right after she pulls out a clump of your hair and punches you in the nose.

Nobody blinks as Jeanine pads back to her desk, wafting her smell behind her, then plops down in her seat. Her dark eyes are as hard as alleys. I look quickly back at Sister. She's wearing a tight smile. I wonder if she likes doing this to Jeanine. But I know that's a very bad thing to think about.

We're all quietly facing the front of the class when Sister drops Jeanine's wad of chewing gum into the wastebasket, then carries on with the lesson.

I know some other bad things about Jeanine Bonenfant. Her family is even poorer than ours. Her mother never gets out of bed. If you walk through the front door of her house, you will see a bed in the living room, with Jeanine's very sick mother slumped on a pillow. She will be buried under sheets that are grayish and used to be white. That's what Monsieur Nadeau, the bread man, has told Maman.

Something is wrong with Madame Bonenfant, but nobody knows what. They say Jeanine's father works hard at his job, but they have even more kids in their family than we do. Eight, I think, but I lost count because it seems like almost every spring there's a new one. Not last spring, though, because she never got out of bed since last winter, Jeanine's mother. Jeanine's older sister, Jacqueline, can't go to school anymore because she has to look after all her younger brothers and sisters. I would hate that.

They also say Jeanine's father is a drunk and sometimes he hits his children, and I think that might be true.

I know Jeanine steals from her mother's purse, which is why she always has money for candy. And coins for the Society of Saint Vincent de Paul charity box too, which helps poor families in our parish without enough food and clothing. I never have any money to give. There is a cardboard box on Sister's desk, a box with a slot in the top, and every day she tells our class about all of those needy people. And every day she instructs her students to bring in some coins to drop into the box for them. Sister says that so many people are "destitute and desperate," and that sometimes their fathers "must resort to begging" in order to feed their families. At our house, there's always enough food for everyone, and we always have clean clothes to wear.

More than anything, I would love to take some coins to my school for those poor, sad families. I would love to be like the other girls in my class who are lucky enough to get to walk up to the front each day and drop a coin through the slot as Sister beams from behind her desk. I would love to be the one everyone watches walking up the aisle to the desk and making the other coins clink when I drop one in. But I am not allowed. There is no change to spare in our family, with so many mouths to feed. Maman doesn't miss a chance to remind us whenever I mention Sister's charity box on her desk. "I have hungry children of my own, tell that to your teacher." But I never will!

Yes, Jeanine is poorer than we are. But she doesn't seem to think so. And that day after school, when she's shuffling along for home in her thick rubber boots with bare feet in them, with NO socks, she lets me know, once again.

"You're so poor that your mother makes your hats," Jeanine yells from the other side of the snowy street. "And you have stinking horses and chickens and a barn in your backyard, and sometimes you even ride to school in a sled!"

My hands turn into fists. Why did she have to say those things to me? I want to run across the street and punch her big nose. Maman has *never* made our hats. She buys us felt hats at the United store for fifty-nine cents. We girls wear store-bought hats in the Sauriol family, not homemade ones like our brothers wear. And those smelly horses and chickens! And the stupid sled that I hate riding in so much. I know I can't punch Jeanine. I'd never win a fight with this girl. I can hit her with words, though. It's my only hope.

"Well you're so poor, your mother makes your stockings!" I holler back at her. "But they're so full of holes that you have to go barefoot in winter because your mother never even gets out of bed to mend them anymore!"

Jeanine shrieks. She takes off running, turns down a side street, and disappears. My cousin Lucille and I link arms and giggle and chatter about what just happened as we wander slowly home, taking a shortcut through a back laneway.

Jeanine steps out from behind a fence and stands there blocking our way. Her coat is too tight across her chest. She isn't wearing mittens, and her hands are red and raw.

"What did you say back there?" If she were a dog she would bite me, I know it.

"Nothing," I tell her as I watch my cousin running away.

"Don't lie to me, Sauriol. I heard what you said," she shrieks again. She grabs me before I have a chance to run. She trips me, knocks off my hat, and yanks on my hair. She kicks great flurries of snow into my face until my mouth and nostrils are full and I'm almost choking. Now she looms over top of me and stares down, her face a tight and fiery mask. She makes a yucky sucking sound in her throat, then lets a long string of snotty drool dribble onto my face. I feel it hot and horrid on my cheek. I want to swipe it away, but I'm too terrified to move. She leans in close. I can feel my heart pounding hard underneath my coat. Maybe she can hear it too, it's so loud in my ears.

"That will teach you to say such stupid things!" Jeanine screams in my face. Then she steps away but keeps on staring at me, her nostrils flaring like a horse, like the two in our yard, where I wish I was.

I lie there, perfectly still, afraid of what she might do next.

"Don't you *ever* talk about me again, or next time it will be even worse for you, Sauriol." Then she adds, "*Maudite habitante*," with a growl.

A damned peasant! Jeanine, the dumb and dirty poor girl from the other side of Scott Street—from Mechanicsville—has called *me* a damned peasant! And spit in my face! For the first time ever, I feel angry enough to kill. Still lying there on the ground, I scrunch up two fistfuls of snow in my quaking hands, then stop, resisting the devil's temptation to sit up and hurl the snow into Jeanine's ugly face. Maybe because my guardian angel is whispering into my ear, knowing I don't stand a chance. "To light and guard, to rule and guide."

I drop the clumps of snow, then stare at the sky, where fat flakes drift to the ground in lazy circles, until I hear her boots churning through the snow and know she's gone. When I finally take a chance, I sit up slowly and wipe the spit from my face with my wet mitten. All I can see is snow and the slanted blue shadows of the houses all around me. Maybe somebody saw what just happened and is laughing behind a curtain in one of the windows. I hate that maybe someone saw Jeanine beating me up, and that maybe they'll tell everyone they know.

I pick myself up and brush myself off, pull on my hat, and scuff my way through the snowy streets the rest of the way home. I try my best to wipe the scowl off my face just before I walk through my back door. Jeanine Bonenfant pushed me down today, but I don't want anyone to know. Oh, but I won't forget this. I will never forget what she just did to me, or the horrible insulting thing she called me. And I *will* find a way to get back at this girl.

3

Four Little Chickens

As soon as I reach Hinchey Avenue, where we live in the Hintonburg neighborhood of Ottawa, across the tracks from the poorer people in Mechanicsville, I start to catch my breath and feel safe again. There are also lots of poor people in our area, which we like to call the Burg. But there are richer people too, a couple of streets over, west of Parkdale. People with nice cars, people with important jobs. The Burg is a better place to live than Mechanicsville, even though we do live close to the tracks.

Whenever I get home from school, there are always good smells coming from the kitchen. No wonder—Maman spends nearly all of her time in there.

"Where's Yvette?" I ask after kicking off my boots.

I stand them up by the door so Papa won't step in a puddle and yell at me when he comes stomping in from outside. He spends lots of time out there—bang, bang, banging on the anvil in the yard, making things and fixing things for people. He makes knives and forks, and resoles our shoes out there too, usually on Saturdays. He also makes horseshoes for our horses.

"Your sister is still in bed," Maman says, and I can tell by the furrows on her face that she's worried. "Still not feeling well after the cold she's had for two weeks."

Or maybe an excuse to stay away from school because she's afraid of Jeanine and her sisters and brothers, I think but don't say out loud. Their whole family is scary. They don't have a Holy Roller like Bernard or a bookworm like Arthur or a quiet sister like Yvette. All of them are like a pack of wild dogs, just waiting to jump on somebody or pelt them with snow or even punch them in the stomach or eye. I've seen it happen. And that snow today was bad enough.

"Where are the boys?" I sniff the air. Raisin pies are cooling. I don't really care where my brothers are right now. All I can think about are those pies.

"Doing their homework in the living room by the fire." Maman sees what I'm looking at. "Have one," she tells me. "Go ahead."

"Really?" I can't believe my luck, but she knows how I love them. "A whole one?"

"*Bien sûr*," she says, then sets a small steaming brown pie on the table and a fork beside it. "I made it just for you, you know. I knew you'd be hungry when you got home. And there are a few more for everyone else to share." I don't waste any time scooping forkfuls of the molten pie into my mouth, not caring how much it burns. I don't want to share this pie that's packed with raisins and a sweet, gooey syrup. I'm eating every bite because Maman said so.

Then I sit in the rocker by the stove, staying warm and reading. It's Papa's chair, but we can use it when he's working outside. He likes it here, after working all day delivering wood and doing odd jobs for people, then hammering on the anvil when he gets home. He sits in this chair to read the paper and to rest, and sometimes even to tell us stories. It's my favorite reading place. As soon as he comes in, though, the chair is his. So when I hear his boots stomp out on the back porch, I jump out of Papa's chair.

Papa's face is red and grim like always. I wonder if he's happy, because he doesn't smile very much. Maman says it's because he has to work so hard to feed his four little chickens, *ses quatre petits poulets*. That's us children—even though we have real chickens out in the henhouse that give us eggs every day.

I don't like the chopping block and axe out there, though.

Once when I was small, I had a pet chicken I named Babette. I chose her when she was just a fluffy, little chick and watched her grow. She was black and would sit on my lap while I stroked her feathers. Then one day when I got home from school and ran to the henhouse, Babette was gone. I didn't eat supper that night, and neither did Maman. And I couldn't eat any chicken for a while after that day, either.

At the table today, Maman and Papa aren't speaking. But I catch them looking at each other. The boys are too busy eating to notice, and Yvette is playing with her food, pushing cabbage around on her plate and not eating. I'm not so hungry now, either, because I know something is wrong. I want to know what it is, but I'm afraid to ask in case it's about the war.

We are afraid of the war. The English, the Americans, and the Canadians are the Allies. And we're fighting enemies. I know about that. Sometimes there are bold headlines in *Le Droit*, our newspaper. Maman, Papa, and Arthur talk about the war in quiet voices. Arthur knows a lot about it, but I don't want to know too much, so I try not to listen. When it all started, I used to catch Maman crying at the stove or while she did the laundry, and I knew something scary happened again. But when she would see me watching, she'd quickly wipe her eyes on her apron and try to smile. A pretend smile, because I knew she was really scared.

Maman loves King George and the Queen Mother and the two princesses, Elizabeth and Margaret, who all live in London, England. She cuts pictures out of the newspaper and glues them into a scrapbook. When they came to Ottawa a few years ago, in 1939, we went to see them, the king and queen. They passed by the corner of Parkdale and Scott Street, so close to our house, and we saw them waving from their big black car.

It was only a few months later, in September, when Britain and France declared war on Germany. Maman started to cry when a neighbor came by to tell us, right after he had heard the news on the radio. Then, when we heard that our prime minister, Mackenzie King, announced that Canada would be joining the war too, Maman cried even more, and I followed her around for three days, holding on to her apron. Yvette didn't care, Bernard prayed, and Arthur studied every single word in the newspaper. As soon as the Germans invaded France and occupied Paris, there was no hiding the worry on her face. Maman says our ancestors are from France and that we still have distant relatives there even though we've never even met them.

When they started dropping bombs on England, Maman cried some more. Then, after the Japanese bombed Pearl Harbor last year and the Americans joined the war, she cried a little bit more. Just for a day or so before she put on her brave face again. But she often says it's terrible what's happening in Europe.

I don't know much about any of it except that bombs are falling and people and soldiers are dying every day. Sometimes I'm glad to be my age because I don't have to know so much about all the awful things that are going on in the world. And I have Jeanine Bonenfant to worry about most of the time now, anyway.

They aren't talking about the war right now, yet Maman and Papa still look very worried. I'm afraid to ask why, so I sit there and wait. Papa puts his fork down and clears his throat, and the others all look at him. Whenever Papa clears his throat that way, it means he's about to say something important to us. And our father doesn't speak very often. So when he does, we're sure to listen.

"We will have tenants living with us. Starting at the end of this month." That's his announcement. I just stare at him because my head is full of questions I'm afraid to ask.

"What does that mean, *tenants*?" Bernard dares to ask, because he's the second youngest and braver because he doesn't know any better yet.

"It means other people who will pay us to live in our house," Arthur explains with a scowl. "So where are *we* supposed to live, Papa?" Arthur is the bravest of all, because he's the oldest and he talks to Papa like a man.

Maman watches our faces. She looks sad but forces a smile, I can tell.

"We will live down here on the bottom floor, and the tenants will live upstairs," she explains. "We'll move our beds down here. They will use our upstairs rooms as their rooms."

"But there's no kitchen up there," Yvette whispers. "I don't want them to eat with us. And I don't want them to eat our pies!"

Maman tries to laugh. "They'll bring along their own things for their kitchen. And their own food. And we'll move some of our furniture upstairs for them to make room for our beds down here. You children will sleep in the front room, and our bedroom will be in the dining room. It will be an adventure. And it will help us; we need more money."

Silence around the table. We always need more money. That's why I can't have coins for the charity box. But what will it be like to have strangers living in our house? Will they use the same bread man and the same milkman as we do? Will Maman have to do their laundry as well as ours? She spends every Monday in the kitchen washing our things in a big tub. On wash day, we have cornflakes for breakfast because Maman is too busy to make porridge. And sometimes before school I help her. I guess I'm not fast enough, though, because she always tells me to stop taking my time. But I can't go any faster than my time, can I?

Maman hangs everything to dry outside, even in winter. Then she carries it all back inside stiff as boards; shirts and dresses that look like flat, invisible people are inside of them until they thaw in the warm kitchen. They smell fresh like outside, all of our clothes and sheets, and I love the smell.

Papa looks stern now, though, so I don't want to ask any questions.

"But what if we don't like them?" Yvette says. "What if they're not nice?"

"They will be nice," Maman says. "*Très gentilles.* Papa and I have met Mr. Coleman already. They're just a mother and father and one little girl named Carolyn. She's younger than Aline and older than Yvette. Bernard's age. They're from London, England. Mr. Coleman has a job here for a short time, and they don't want to buy a house. He's staying at a hotel right now, and his family will arrive soon from London."

"Will they talk funny?" Bernard asks. "Will they talk French like us? I don't know much English yet."

Neither do I, but I know more than Bernard. We're learning it in school now. Some of my friends are better at it than I am, though, because they have an English parent or neighbors on their street or even English friends. So they get a chance to practice sometimes. But at the library, I try to read English books sometimes, for the practice.

"Will she go to school with us?" Yvette says. "I don't want her to."

"*Non*, ma belle. They are Protestants," Maman tells her, and Yvette and Bernard gasp.

"I don't want Protestants to live here," Yvette says, beginning to cry. Arthur grins at that. "Protestants aren't like us. They're bad. And sometimes they throw snowballs at us on the way home from school."

"So do the Bonenfants, and they're good Catholics like you," Arthur reminds her with a smirk. "You don't have to be a Protestant to act stupid, you know."

Maman shakes her head. "They're not bad, *les Protestants*," she explains. "They have a different church and say their Mass in a different way, that's all. And their priests can get married, not like ours. And Carolyn will go to the English school, not to your school. Okay?"

"Uh-oh. Will they bring the Blitz here with them?" Bernard asks, his eyes wide.

We all know what the Blitz is as it happened just last year. A lot of people in Britain died and a lot of their buildings and houses were destroyed by bombs. But when Arthur just shakes his head, rolls his eyes, and groans, that means Bernard said something silly. I'm glad because I was almost worried about the same thing as my younger brother.

"Of course not, Bernard." Papa heaves a huge sigh and grumbles. "Enough questions for now. Just wait and see, *les enfants*, wait and see," he tells us. "Not long until they arrive at the beginning of December, and we have lots to do before then to get our house ready. And you will all help out with that. Correct?"

We all nod. We know there is no other choice.

"*Bon*," he says, with a half-smile. "Almost time for prayers. Finish your supper, and when Maman has cleaned up the kitchen, we will gather around the table once more."

We nod again. We say our prayers together every night. I'm not sure Maman is that fond of it. Her face always looks tight when we do it, and during the rosary she says her Hail Marys very fast, like she wants the prayers to be over soon. Sometimes I'm pretty sure she wishes she could be doing something else. Busy Maman always has something to do, no matter what time of day. But Papa won't allow her to knit or darn socks or sew while we're praying.

Tonight, I'm praying that the Coleman family from England really will be a very nice family, like Maman said. Très gentille. And that they won't feel sorry for us because of everything that we don't have, which is why we need to rent rooms to them in the first place. I almost feel silly to be praying for something so foolish instead of devoting my prayers to asking God if he will please bring a quick end to the horrible war that has the whole world living in terror. But I don't know very much about the war. What I do know is that in a few weeks our lives here on Hinchey Street in the Burg will change in a very big way.

"Wait and see, children," Papa has told us. That won't be easy. I always find it very hard waiting. For anything.

4

Just One Dime

That night, I dream of hungry babies, crying and reaching out their tiny hands. Everyone in my class is there with me and has money to give them. Even Jeanine. But I don't have a single coin to give them because I have no money. I never have any money. Maman keeps it in her purse, high on a shelf in the cupboard. She uses her money to pay the bread man and the milkman, and to go to the market.

It was a bad dream, but in the morning I have a good idea that might really work. Papa is outside already, and Maman is somewhere else in the house. Yvette is still in bed, and Arthur is in the bathroom. *What about the bathroom?* I wonder suddenly, sitting there at the table with Bernard, who pretends to eat his porridge. *Will we have to share ours with the Colemans?*

No time to worry about that now, though. I have a plan, and I have to hurry. It's almost easy to ignore my guardian angel, who whispers warnings into my ear about what I'm doing wrong this time. What difference will one penny make to our family when Sister has told us that it will help to put food on another family's table? And maybe someday I'll find the courage to tell Maman what I did, and maybe she'll understand.

I push a sturdy kitchen chair over to the counter. Bernard frowns when I climb up, so I touch my finger to my lips.

"Shhh, Bernard," I tell him. "*Ne dis rien*. Don't say a word. I'm getting a penny to take to Sister for the church charity box. It's a good thing to do. We have to try to help the poor and hungry families." Bernard nods solemnly. "You stand by the window and tell me if Papa is coming, okay?" He nods again and hurries to the window.

I stand on the counter and pull Maman's purse out of the cupboard where she keeps it hidden. My quick fingers twist open the little brass balls on the change purse and dig through the coins. I know I have to hurry when I hear Maman's footsteps on the stairs. I can't even look inside the purse. I just snatch one small coin, snap the little purse shut, and put it back. I move the chair and sit down at the table to finish my porridge, just in time. But Bernard stands there with wide eyes and mouth too.

"*Quoi*?" Maman asks. "What's wrong here?"

"*Rien*," I tell her. "Nothing, Maman. Sit down and finish your porridge, Bernard," I tell my brother in a helpful older-sister way. He stares at me as he sits down, and Maman watches both of us. Then she shrugs her shoulders and carries on with her housework, disappearing down the steps into the cold cellar, where she stores her tins and jars of pickles and fruits.

"*Tu vois*," I whisper, holding out one small coin for my brother to see, then realizing it's not a penny at all. Now even more families will be fed and clothed. "It's just one little dime. Ten cents. Maman won't mind." I hope I'm right. And I put my finger against my lips again.

The dime is clutched tightly in my hand. It will stay there until I can march up the aisle like all the other girls have done already, drop it into Sister's charity box, and finally hear it go clink with all the other coins. Finally, I can help support some poor people!

All the way to school, the dime stays in my hand. It's there inside my blue woolen mitten that Maman knit for me. Yes, she knits our mittens, but she buys our hats! Yvette has come to school today too, even though she's still coughing. But I have that coin, solid and warm in my hand, for the starving babies that I dreamed about, so nothing else matters. I can't wait to drop the ten cents into Sister's charity box.

But when I get there, when I hang all my things in the cloakroom and hurry to the front of the classroom where Sister is sitting at her desk—oh no, oh no! The charity box is gone!

"Quoi, Aline?" Sister asks in her impatient voice as hard lines form on her face. "Can I help you with something?" It will not be a good day for the students if Sister starts the day off mad because of me. Jeanine Bonenfant is bad enough, and she hasn't even arrived yet. On most days, she can make Sister Madeleine angry before she even gets to school.

"*La boite*," I finally manage to say. "The charity box for the poor. Where is it?" I hold out the coin in my damp hand.

"It's gone already, Aline," she tells me in a too-loud voice that I'm afraid everyone will hear. "It's been picked up. You're too late. Take your money home."

Some snickers come from behind me, but they stop the instant Sister raises a scary black eyebrow. I don't even want to turn around to see the faces of the girls who might be laughing at me for being too late, for missing my chance to help. Instead, I lower my eyes and shuffle to my desk. I wish I could crawl inside of it to hide.

Then the door slams open at the back of the classroom. It's Jeanine Bonenfant, late again. All heads turn, including mine, and Sister starts to yell, tells Jeanine to stay in the cloakroom instead of going to her desk. Nobody cares about me anymore.

I feel like thanking Jeanine when I see her furious face peering from underneath the cloakroom door, sticking her tongue out at the world. Because today, she saved me.

The dime stays in my left hand all day: through prayers and lessons and sums; when I look, secretly, while Sister writes on the blackboard, there is a small circle in my skin, I've held on to the dime so tightly. It stays there all the way home for lunch as the church bells ring out the Angelus, which reminds me to say a little prayer in my heart; all through eating my pea soup and bread; and all the way back to school again, it's still there. I don't know what to do with the dime. I'm afraid to put it back in case Maman or Papa or even Arthur catches me. All the icy boldness that I found this morning has melted away. Now I'm just a wet puddle.

By the time the last bell rings and I meet my cousin Lucille in the schoolyard, I know exactly what I have to do next. I link arms with her as we leave, and I make her walk fast so that Yvette won't catch up. My sister always walks so slowly, and I don't want her to know about the money.

When we're far enough away, I take my mitten off and open my hand.

"Look," I tell Lucille. She stares at the coin with her pink mouth and chestnut-colored eyes wide open. Her red felt hat is tied up under her chin, and her dark bangs hang in her eyes. There's a small drip on the end of her nose that looks pretty even though it's snot. Lucille always looks pretty. I never do.

Even though our fathers are brothers, they don't really look alike. How can two brothers have completely different noses? And why can't my nose be nice and round like Lucille's and Uncle Pierre's? And why can't Papa be more like my uncle?

I sometimes wish that Lucille's father was my father instead because whenever I see him, he's smiling. But I always say a prayer to Sainte-Thérèse after having such bad thoughts. Papa says his brother isn't worth talking to and neither is anyone else in his family. *Mon oncle* can't be that bad, though, if he's always smiling. Sometimes I hear my aunt yelling through the open windows in summer, and Lucille says her parents have fights now and then. I'd like a smiling father, but I wouldn't like a fighting one.

"Where did you get that?" Lucille asks, and I explain about the poor families and Maman's change purse in the cupboard.

"I wanted to help them," I tell her when her face gets serious. "But Maman said no. So I took the money anyway. Don't tell anybody."

"You'll have to tell that at confession. Stealing is a sin," Lucille reminds me.

As if I didn't think of that already myself. "Is it a sin even if it's to help somebody poorer than you, though?" I wonder out loud.

"Maybe not, but it is if you keep it for yourself, isn't it?"

"I don't know," I tell her. Neither of us are sure about sins, the big mortal ones or the smaller venial ones. Sometimes it seems that everything is a sin, everything we secretly think or do. Sometimes I think that the devil is sitting on my shoulder telling me to do bad things and that my guardian angel isn't doing her job very well.

"Maman gave me a penny for the box a couple of times," Lucille tells me. "Never that much, though." She touches the coin in my hand.

"Is it a lot?" I ask her. I know about money, but I have no idea how much this one can buy. It's a dime, with a picture of the king on one side and a boat on the other.

"Ten cents? I think so," Lucille tells me. "Maybe you should just give it back."

"But if Papa finds out…" I stop right there because I don't even dare to imagine what might happen. "I know what! Let's go to the store instead and buy some candy!"

Lucille's eyes get wide and bright.

"Really! You mean it, Aline?"

Neither of us ever has money to go to the store, unless it's to buy something for our mothers, like rice or peas or bread. How can she say no? And she doesn't. She just stands there smiling and nodding. We both forget about sins for now and make a beeline for the five-and-dime.

5

Ten Cents' Worth

"A nd what can I do for you today, little girls?" asks the fat man with the red face who is leaning over the counter.

Lucille and I can't even speak. We just press our faces to the glass for a closer look at everything we never get to have. Frosty gumdrops, square brown caramels, long licorice whips, taffy, peppermints, humbugs, and lollipops. And chocolates.

"Noses and fingers off the glass," the man grumbles. "Do you know how often I have to wipe those glass windows because of all the grubby little fingers and noses touching them?"

Lucille steps back. I hope she doesn't start to cry like she sometimes does. I step forward and put the dime on the counter.

"Could we have some candy, please?" I ask in my politest voice.

Now he's smiling. "Of course you can. What would you like?"

My heart is beating hard, and I wonder if my guardian angel

is frowning beside me. She can't be very happy about this black mark that is sure to appear on my soul. I start to feel a bit sick inside my heart, but I sweep the feelings away like Maman does with crumbs on the floor.

"Anything," I tell him.

"Ten cents' worth?" he asks, and I just nod dumbly as he starts to fill a paper bag.

When the bag is half full I start to feel even sicker. "You can stop now," I tell him.

"A few more to go, for a dime's worth," he tells me and drops even more in with some long spoons that are stuck together on one end. When I look to my side, Lucille's not there. When I look over my shoulder, I see her moving slowly backward to the doorway as if we're stealing this candy and not buying it. Are we? Because I took the coin from Maman's purse?

"Here you go," the fat man says and hands me the bag.

I run out the door into the snowy day as if I really did steal the candy. Lucille is out there looking very scared now. But she looks interested too. She wants me to open that bag just as much as I want me to open it. We slip down a laneway and stare at each other.

"It's so full," I whisper. "I wonder if he made a mistake." I uncrumple the top of the bag and open it so we can both see inside. We both sniff the sweetness. It even smells delicious.

"You go first," I tell her, holding out the bag.

My cousin reaches inside and pulls out three gumdrops: a red, a green, and a yellow. She quickly shoves them into her mouth, then looks all around in case someone is watching. She starts to chew and closes her eyes and smiles.

I reach in and pull out a caramel. In my mouth, it's sweet and chewy and creamy, and sticks to my teeth. Before it's gone, I shove in a piece of chocolate. Chocolate and caramel mixed together is heavenly. I can't stop smiling.

"Your teeth are brown," Lucille tells me, and we both start giggling like mad.

Then we start to stuff our faces, but before I know it, Lucille is bent over and crying.

"My tummy hurts," she whines. "I don't want any more."

I feel the same way. And there's still more than half a bag of candy left. I don't want to keep it, but I don't want to throw it away, either. Maman says it's a waste to throw things away. She uses every single scrap. It's almost like magic. The quilts on our beds are made of clothes from when we were little. She turns too-small sweaters into socks and bread crusts into bread pudding. Vegetable scraps go into the soup pot. Old shoes come back to life with new soles. Sometimes even the too-small bits of leftover pie dough get rolled up with brown sugar and butter, and baked into *des pets de sœurs*—nun's farts—and they are so delicious!

But how do I dare take this candy home knowing that I've committed a sin?

"Here, you have it." I push the paper bag toward Lucille's hands, but her face looks funny now, and she pushes it back. She folds over even more, making a funny gagging noise. Suddenly, she throws up all over her boots. All the candy she just finished chewing. And then she begins to cry, of course.

"*T'es méchante*, Aline," she sobs, wiping her mouth on her sleeve. "You're bad. You made me eat all that candy that you bought with money you stole from your maman."

"Maudit, maudit, maudit," I mutter, and my cousin gasps because I've said damn out loud. Three times! And now I will surely wind up in limbo for eternity with all the pagans instead of heaven. I know that's exactly what she's thinking—the same as me.

I hear Jeanine say it all the time, though, and worse things too, and she doesn't seem to worry about eternity. And it almost feels good to say those words out loud because I'm so mad right now. It pops my madness like a soap bubble and helps me feel better. But I'd never tell anyone that. I shove the bag of leftover candy into the bottom of my schoolbag.

"*Dis rien à ta mère*," I warn Lucille. "Don't tell your mother what happened, okay?"

She nods like crazy, then I help her clean the rainbow of sick off her boots with some handfuls of snow. As we walk slowly the rest of the way home, I ask God and my guardian angel to forgive me for being such a bad, bad girl today.

"And anyway," I say to Lucille when we're almost there and she doesn't look so ill anymore, "Jeanine Bonenfant steals from her sick mother's purse, like I told you before. And even from her father's pockets. She always has candy, and money for the charity box."

"And that means she'll go to hell," Lucille murmurs. "Forever and ever."

"Because she does it every day," I add, not even certain that what I'm saying is true. "And I only ever did it one time. And I'm never doing it again." I know that much is true.

"Will you tell the priest what you did at confession?" Lucille asks, her eyes wider now.

I smile and nod at my cousin. But that nod might be a lie. Another sin now for my poor broken soul. And there's still the candy at the bottom of my schoolbag. I can't throw it away because that would be a sin too. I have to find a place to hide it that nobody will think of.

I think I know just the place. Only God and my guardian angel will see me put it there. And I hope they won't be too unhappy with me.

On Saturday morning when I kneel down in the confessional and wait for our priest, Father Louis, to slide open the little door, I can feel myself shaking. I'm holding on to a sin, and I know I have to confess what I did sooner or later. The bag of candy is in my secret hiding place inside my house. Yvette was allowed to come to church with me because it's not so cold out as usual today. She's already been to confession and waits, praying, in a pew. *What sins could Yvette have committed?* I can't help but wonder. She's been sick and housebound for so long now. Her soul must still be sin-free from the last time she went to Father Louis for forgiveness.

Today, after Papa delivers his wood, we are moving all our bedroom things from upstairs to downstairs, and some of our living room and dining room things upstairs. The renters from England will be here soon, and I'm not sure if I'm worried or excited about that. But before anything else happens, I have to confess my sins. When the little door opens and I can see the dim outline of Father's face, I begin. I try to breathe through my mouth so I won't have to sniff his stinky breath. And then I start my confession, speaking much faster than usual.

"Bless me Father for I have sinned. It has been one week since my last confession, and these are my sins: I said mean things to my sister, I made fun of a girl at school, I had bad thoughts after that girl kicked snow in my face, and I disobeyed Maman and Papa."

And that's where I stop. Because I just can't say what else I did. And when I really think about it, I "disobeyed" my parents by taking that coin out of Maman's purse. There isn't enough time to tell the whole story. Others are waiting behind me to polish their souls. I kneel there, waiting for my penance. I hope Father can't read my mind like God can. And I hope God understands why I did this, why I'm too ashamed of myself to tell the whole story.

The Act of Contrition, three Hail Marys, and an Our Father. That's my penance today after Father Louis forgives and blesses me. The same as I always get from him. I scurry out from behind the confessional curtain with my hands folded in a pious way and my head bowed. I slip into the pew beside Yvette, who is still kneeling and murmuring into her hands. I begin to pray, thinking how hard it must be to become a saint, like Sainte Thérèse de Lisieux, who lived in France a long time ago and saw a statue of the Virgin Mary smile once when she was sick. I've stared at a statue of the Blessed Virgin in our church for hours, and she has never smiled at me. I glance up at the crucifix that towers over the altar. Jesus Christ always looks so sad, with his head slumped to one side and all those bleeding wounds. The ones he got for saving our wicked human souls. And as usual, I feel guilty for not trying hard enough to be good. As I begin to pray, I promise poor dead Jesus that I will be better this coming week. I will make a fresh start, starting right now.

Mon Dieu, j'ai un très grand regret. O my God, I am heartily sorry for having offended Thee, says the repentant voice in my head.

And it's not until I'm halfway home, with Yvette dragging along behind me, that I realize I forgot one sin. A very big one. I forgot to tell Father Louis that I said a bad word three times in a row. Not such a good start to the week after all. I'm hungry, and I'm disappointed with myself, and I just want to get home for lunch, but Yvette is so slow.

When I turn around to tell her to hurry up, I spot someone coming around the corner: Jeanine Bonenfant. She's got one of her little brothers by the wrist, and she's half dragging him. He's crying and fighting with her and trying to get loose, struggling like an angry cat. I can hear her yelling at him, telling him that he has to go home. I catch hold of Yvette's hand and pull her closer to me as if I'm already trying to protect her.

"There's Jeanine," I lean in and whisper. "She's such an awful girl. *Détestable!* And she hates me. And I don't even know why."

And right at that instant, Jeanine looks over and spots us, and her face becomes a grimace.

"What are you looking at, maudite habitante? Are you talking about me again? To your stupid sister who's always sick? You better watch your step, Sauriol. I hope you can run fast."

"Oh no! Let's run home. Please, Aline." Yvette tugs on my arm. She's close to tears.

But all I can think about is the way Jeanine knocked me down and the hot spit on my cheek, dripping out of her ugly mouth. And how she just called me "maudite habitante," words I despise. And then I say it, because I can't hold it inside anymore.

"You are a horrible girl, Bonenfant," I yell at her. "No wonder your mother is always sick! You're probably the one who makes her sick. You will never *ever* go to heaven."

"*Ferme ta gueule.*" Shut your trap, she says. Then she lets out a howl of rage and starts to charge straight at us. Her little brother isn't crying anymore. He's running now too. They're both chasing after us, and we won't stand a chance against these two Bonenfant children who are acting like crazy animals, like mad dogs.

Yvette and I start running then too. Poor Yvette is having trouble keeping up with me. She can't help it, not being well at all lately. I can hear her coughing and sputtering, and I grab hold of her hand and pull her along behind me. All my good intentions have been crushed. All my prayers for redemption don't even count anymore because I've taunted this awful girl. But I couldn't help it because she is so mean and her soul must be as black as coal. And it's true, she'll never go to heaven. She'll be stuck in purgatory forever.

Home is close, but not close enough. Snowballs whiz past our ears now and smash on the road ahead of us. If it were summer, they would throw rocks; there is always ammunition for the Bonenfant children to hurl at everyone they hate.

"Hurry," I tell my sister. "If she catches us we are finished."

Yvette, her face all red, is bawling now. It's all she has left inside her. I take a chance and glance over my shoulder to check how close they are. And there, gliding along the road, is a most wonderful sight. It's Papa and his sled, coming home from delivering wood today. Jeanine sees him too, and stops dead in her sloppy galoshes.

"Look! It's the stupid habitant sled," she yells, and she and her brother start laughing.

But I don't care. I've never been so happy to see our papa and his sled and horses.

"*Bonjour, mes belles filles*," he calls as the sled shudders to a stop beside us. Yvette and I clamber into the back atop the hay, Papa shakes the reins, and the sled slides off toward home.

When I peer over the back, Jeanine and her brother are still pointing and laughing at us.

6

Blue Mittens

The upstairs of our house looks strange. After church on Sunday, Maman, Yvette, and I walk through the bedrooms that once were ours. Our tenants, les Protestants, as I've come to think of them, will be here next Saturday, just three days before the calendar turns into December.

Now we have bedrooms instead of a living room and dining room. And upstairs, in Maman and Papa's old bedroom, is all our furniture: the chesterfield and armchair and small tables as well as the dining room table and chairs. It looks silly and sad at the same time, all squashed together in this not-so-big room. Maman stands in the upstairs hallway with her hands on her hips, looking in the boys' bedroom, where the Coleman family will sleep. They will bring along their own beds that they've purchased here in Canada, Maman tells us, as well as a stove to cook on and an icebox. Their kitchen will be in the third bedroom, mine and

✳ 47 ✳

Yvette's. It didn't take Papa and Arthur too long to move things around today. Yvette and I tried to carry a small table up the stairs, and Papa made a face when we dented the wall. Then he told us not to help anymore.

"They should be very comfortable up here," Maman says with a sigh. "And now we have a week to get used to the new arrangements before they move in. You girls and your brothers will be fine down in the living room, and Papa and I in the dining room. We have our nice big kitchen for sitting and eating in. And they will use our bathroom. It won't be for too long. Just until things get a bit better."

What things? I want to ask, but I don't dare. Yvette has tears in her eyes.

"Will Papa still tell us *les contes* about Ti-Jean?" she asks. We love it when Papa tells stories about the little boy who always gets into mischief.

"Bien sûr!" Maman smiles. "Of course. In the kitchen by the stove, like always."

"Where will we go to the bathroom and take a bath?" Yvette asks in her almost-crying voice. Her mouth is beginning to tremble and droop. She's asking the silliest questions, but I don't mind because it saves me from asking the same ones myself.

Maman chuckles a little. "We can use the bathtub and the bathroom whenever they're not using it. They won't always be using it, ma belle."

"*J'aime pas ça*," Yvette murmurs, then stomps her foot.

I don't like it, either, strangers living in our bedrooms and nine people sharing one bathroom. But I don't want to tell Maman and hurt her feelings.

"*Nous n'avons pas le choix*, Yvette," Maman says in a stiff voice before she spins around and clomps down the stairs in her heavy black shoes. We have no choice, she says.

We don't have much choice about anything in our house, I can't help but think. My friend Georgette has lots of choices, including two kinds of store-bought cookies—Peek Freans and Dad's—that we get to eat when I go to her house. She's plump, with pink cheeks. She gets to pick out her own clothes downtown at Ogilvy's too. I've never been there in my life. And I can't remember ever having a choice in my life, either. Except for my blue mittens. Yvette got the red ones.

At school, the only person I tell is my cousin Lucille. And I beg her to please not tell anyone because I'm so ashamed that we will have another family, a Protestant family, living with us. That must mean we're very poor, and I hate being very poor. Well, not hate, because hating anything is a sin, so instead I detest it.

All through class on Monday afternoon, Jeanine Bonenfant stares at me with narrow slits for eyes. She's already gotten the strap twice today and is in a nasty mood. When I look at her, she makes a slashing motion at her neck then points at me, and I gulp hard. Why is she so mad at me? I haven't even said a single word to her today. I know I should have kept my mouth shut when I saw her on Saturday and she chased us, but my boiling anger wouldn't let me even though I'd just been to confession to cleanse my grimy soul. Can she still be mad about that, even though she and her brother laughed at us?

After school, I'm afraid to leave, so instead I stay to help Sister clean off the blackboard. I love doing that anyway, watching all the letters and numbers disappear as I make slow circles with my arm, then going outside and banging the brushes on the wall. Afterward, Sister asks me to write some arithmetic problems on the blackboard for tomorrow. I love writing with chalk, skating it over the black slate and taking my time to make every single number perfect.

By the time I'm finished and heading for home, the afternoon light is starting to fade. Snow falls in a thick veil, covering everything so fast that it's hard to see ahead of me through the blur. I keep my head low so the snow won't get in my eyes. I kick a chunk of ice and watch it slide ahead of me on the frozen pavement—until it gets stopped by a pair of battered rubber boots covering a pair of huge feet. I look up. Jeanine Bonenfant's hands are on her hips and her eyes are narrow slits, her angry face a twisted mask.

"Is it true? You told people I steal from *ma mère*?" she growls.

Suddenly I feel very hot under my coat. The only people I told are my cousin Lucille and my friend Thérèse. But I know Thérèse has a very big mouth and probably told some of her other friends, and then one of them said something to somebody else. And somehow or other, Jeanine heard about it. And now I'm a dead duck. It doesn't matter what I say. Either answer will be the wrong one. So I make my choice.

"*Oui*," I tell her, trying to make my face hard and tough. "Because you do. That's why you always have money for candy. And for Sister's charity box."

Her horse nostrils flare like last time. Her mean mouth is a tight white line. Inside dark circles like bruises, her eyes are cruel slits. She takes a step toward me. I watch her slowly raise her hand, and I draw in a quick breath. Then her hand flies out and she slaps my face so hard that it makes me wince, and sudden tears jump into my eyes.

I don't move even though I would like so much to soothe the wicked stinging on my cheek with my cold mitten. Maybe I'm too scared, or maybe I want to pretend I'm not as scared as I really am. But I'm so frightened that I can feel myself quaking, and I'm sure my guardian angel must be too. I don't feel her guarding me very well right now, either.

"Take back what you said," she growls in my face. "Take it back."

"I won't," I tell her. Nothing matters right now. Nothing will change her mind.

I fear what might happen next, but it still takes me by surprise. When Jeanine begins to punch my stomach with tight, strong fists, my breath is gone. Each sharp jab is a blow like I've never felt in my life. Like nobody should ever feel. In another instant, I fold in half and topple over as hot tears finally burst from my eyes. Jeanine kicks a chunk of ice at me and, with one last sneer, jumps over a snowbank and disappears into the twilight, leaving me sitting there on the ground in the falling snow, sucking in great gulps of air. And moaning with a new ache that I've never felt in my life. Because I know somebody utterly hates me.

I don't hurry to get home. I slip-slide along through the tumbling snow in my old boots, going slowly, wishing for the ache in my stomach to stop. I pass a group of boys playing hockey on the road with a frozen horse ball. They make good pucks. I see some laughing rosy-faced children I know coming back from sledding. They wave at me. I wish I could be having fun like them instead of feeling so sick inside.

I stop just outside the back door to make sure my tears are all gone, one last wipe with my blue mitten. Good smells are coming through the door. I can hear my family talking in there, Papa's gruff voice. He's already inside for supper, which means I'm later than usual. As soon as I step inside, all heads turn at once.

"You're late," Maman says, frowning. She's holding a pot of potatoes in one hand and a big spoon in the other. Then she frowns even deeper. "What happened, Aline?"

"Rien," I tell her. Nothing. Which is a lie, so I've sinned again this week. "I was helping Sister after school, that's all." At least that part is true, so I try to smile.

Maman just nods, though I think she must know that there's more I'm not telling. But how does she know? How can she tell that something really is wrong? I try not to look at them all as I take off my boots and hang my coat on the hooks by the door. We are having pork and turnip tonight with the potatoes. I don't like turnip, but I'm too hungry to care and don't even look up as I swallow my food without even tasting it.

Jeanine Bonenfant beat me up today. The girl who is even poorer than we are. The girl who lives in Mechanicsville, on the other side of the railroad tracks. The girl who sometimes has bruises on her arms and bugs in her hair and a dirty neck. The girl who seems happy to beat up anyone. And who steals money from her sick mother's purse. Like I did myself. So I'm really not much better than she is.

That night, in bed beside Yvette, I hear the train pass, a lonely distant whistle blast and the *clickety-clack* of the wheels on the tracks. It helps me fall asleep most nights. But tonight, I can't stop thinking about Jeanine sleeping at her house on the other side of those tracks, with her Maman in a bed in the living room and her father who's a drunk, like people say. And all her grubby brothers and sisters. Jeanine Bonenfant, who is always mad at everyone, it seems.

At least we own our house. Papa built it himself years and years ago when Arthur and I were very small, before Bernard and Yvette were born. It's strong and sturdy, made from fieldstones that he collected, Maman has told us, by taking his horse and wagon out and picking every single one himself, down by the river and over in Tunney's Pasture. Jeanine lives in a messy, dirty house, I've heard tell. I have never been to her house, and I never want to go there, either. She'll never be my friend and I don't care, because I have Lucille, and Thérèse too, with her garage and car. And Georgette, who always has nice shoes and clothes to wear and a telephone in her house. And probably hot water too, whenever they turn on the tap. We have to heat our water in a tank beside the stove before our baths. The rest of the time it comes out cold. Georgette's father has a job delivering fruit and vegetables to grocery stores, so they always have money too. And we don't.

I like my house, even though we can only use half of it now and tenants will be living in the other half soon. I like my bed, even though it's in the living room now. I wish we weren't poor, though. I wish Papa didn't scowl so much. I wish we had bright shiny new things like some others do. I wish for a lot of things that I know will never come true. Especially the one for an "English" nose.

For the rest of the week, I stay far away from Jeanine. I don't look at her, and I don't talk about her, and I don't tell a soul what she did to me. Sometimes when I peek, though, I catch her staring at me. And she has a funny look on her face, like she's daring me to try something like that again. Because next time will be even worse than the last two times.

The best part of every day is recess because it has snowed so much. We build ice slides out in the schoolyard and glide back and forth. Some girls build *bonhommes de neige,* snowmen, and others have snowball fights in the far corner of the schoolyard. Jeanine Bonenfant plays in that corner, with some of the other big, tough girls. Big, tough, dumb girls who should be in Grade 8 or 9, but are only in Grade 6 or 7 because they hardly ever come to school and always fail. I try to stay far away from those girls. Instead, I fool around in the snow with Georgette and Lucille and Thérèse, who has the same name as my favorite saint, who saw the Virgin Mary smile, who was small and perfect and called "The Little Flower." I don't think there's a Sainte Adéline, and there probably never will be. And I'm not small and perfect at all.

We have so much fun playing in the snow on Friday. We make snowballs because the snow is so soft and wet, and throw them at one another, but not so hard that it hurts. We laugh and scream and run around the schoolyard chasing and tripping one another like all the other girls when suddenly, a hard smack in the back of my head almost knocks me over. It knocks my hat off, though, and stings so much that tears jump into my eyes.

When I spin around, I can see Jeanine across the schoolyard, laughing like crazy with her ugly friends, her ugly mouth wide open, and her ugly head thrown back.

"Your mother makes your hats, habitante," she yells, and I cringe when everyone looks. "Your family lives like farm peasants! In a dirty barnyard full of horseshit!"

"Détestable," I mutter. I wish I could shove a snowball down her ugly throat even though that's a bad wish. Instead, I scoop up a handful of snow and start packing it, good and hard. It becomes a tight, icy ball as I rub it in my bare hands. Georgette has picked up my hat and the mittens that I just dropped, and she's staring at me wide-eyed, like Lucille and Thérèse.

"Aline, don't do it," she warns me, but I'm furious now. I don't know how I can possibly stop myself from doing it. My arm starts to rise on its own as if I have no control. Which I don't, because my guardian angel is losing and the devil is winning. And that snowball feels so solid and dangerous in my hand, with the icy burn on my bare skin.

But just as the devil is about to throw it, something happens. I see Jeanine's hand in the air and a quick white blur of something flying straight toward my head. And my guardian angel tells me to duck, so I do. Just in time to see it whiz past my face. Just in time to see Sister Marie, the principal, step out the school doors to ring her bell and summon us inside.

And a whack! And a shriek! Snow is all over Sister's habit and dripping from her very red face. I drop my snowball and crush it under my boot. Everyone starts pointing toward Jeanine, including me and my friends, because—mon Dieu—we sure don't want to be blamed for this one!

"Jeanine Bonenfant!" Sister Marie yells in her scariest of scary voices.

And everyone in the schoolyard freezes.

7

We Like Cabbage

When Jeanine shuffles past me toward the school doors, I hear her mutter the word under her breath. It's a word that we *never* say. The most terrible horrible word in the world.

"*Tabarnac*," she says so we girls can all hear. Which is a slang word for tabernacle. Which is where Jesus lives in the church. Which is an awful sin when you use it to swear. We all gasp at once. Sister Marie hasn't heard, though, which is a good thing. She's already gone inside to wait in her office with her strap.

Then Jeanine says something else, just as she passes me.

"*Tu vas payer,* A-de-line Sau-ri-ol," she hisses, and I can't help but shiver.

I will pay for this? What did I do? I can't understand this girl at all and the way she's started to blame me for all her woes. And saying awful things about me and my family. She is méchante! Bad, bad, bad, in every way. But at least she will get the strap to pay for all her sins. We quietly file into the school a few minutes later. As we walk past Sister's office, we hear it. That sharp whack of the leather strap on the palms of someone's hands. We all know who that someone is. And something in my stomach twists with the sound of every smack.

Jeanine is quiet for the rest of the day. She's slumped over her desk, which Sister Madeleine has moved to the very back corner of the classroom, with her face buried in her arms. Sister carries on with her lessons, probably happy that Jeanine is behaving for a change. I wonder if she's asleep as I pad to the back of the classroom in my stocking feet to sharpen my pencil before we do our arithmetic. Then I realize she's not sleeping at all when I hear the softest of sniffles.

Can it be true? Can Jeanine Bonenfant actually be crying?

"Your house smells of cabbage. Did you know that, little girl?" That's the very first thing Carolyn Coleman says to me on Saturday after they've moved in. And she's littler than I am, well younger, anyway, but taller, so she called me little girl!

Our house really does smell like cabbage, I guess. We eat a lot of it. But the first thing I say to Carolyn Coleman is this: "We like cabbage. And you're littler than I am, you know. And we don't want to play with you, me and my sister, Yvette," I tell her in my slow broken English. "You're a Protestant."

She doesn't cry. She doesn't even get mad. Instead, Carolyn Coleman laughs in a silvery way that reminds me of bells.

"I don't care," she says. "I like being alone. Me and my dollies. They make me happy." Then she clatters up the stairs in her shiny black shoes with the heels that click and disappears into the bedroom that only last week I shared with Yvette.

Yvette and I hid in the living room, our bedroom now, and watched as two men moved the Colemans' things upstairs. There was a big trunk, probably for their clothes, and some things for the kitchen, like a small stove and an icebox. Our "icebox" is a cupboard outside on the back porch. And Carolyn has at least three different dolls wearing lovely clothes. I saw her carrying them up the stairs like babies. And then one of the men carried up a white bassinet—she even has a beautiful bed for her dolls. Papa made us a crib for ours out of wood scraps from our backyard.

Madame Coleman is very pretty. Carolyn looks just like her. And they both have beautiful coats; Carolyn's is navy plaid, and Madame Coleman's black one looks like a wooly lamb and has a fur collar. And they both have turned up English noses and lovely hair as shiny and brown and smooth as chestnuts. And dimples when they smile. They each smiled as they passed on the stairs and spotted my sister and me spying on them. They pretended they didn't see, but I know they did. Monsieur Coleman is tall and thin too, with a thin mustache and nose, and even thin hair. I can see the top of his shiny head. Not like Papa, who has thick dark

---

hair like a bear, Maman says. Mr. Coleman smiled and nodded too, when he passed by on the stairs and saw us watching.

Maybe the Colemans will be nice, but I'm not sure yet. And Carolyn told me that our house smells like cabbage, then she made a yucky face. She has dolls, though, and I wish I could hold one of them, they look so pretty. Yvette and I each have one doll. We've played with them so much that their faces look funny now, squashed in places. And Yvette's doll has only one eye left, which looks scary, but she still loves her. Our dolls don't have real hair like Carolyn's. They have hair that's hard, just like their faces. And they have soft cloth bodies that flop around. Carolyn's dollies look very stiff.

All of a sudden, everything seems different at home. Whenever we make noise, my sister and brothers and I, Maman puts a finger against her lips and says, "Shhh." She never used to do that before today, and now we have to spend the rest of Saturday learning to be quieter in our own house. We don't slide down the banister anymore when Maman isn't looking, or run, shrieking, from room to room playing chase. Yet the Colemans don't have to be quiet upstairs.

We can hear music playing. That's because they have a radio. What must it be like to have your very own radio in the house? Maman says someday, but right now we have a house to pay for and we can't afford to have a "luxury" like a radio, and isn't it far better to have your own house than to have your own radio? Now we get to listen to the Colemans' radio, so that's the first nice thing about them living here. Sometimes I can hear Madame Coleman singing along with the songs on the radio in a sweet voice.

But we can hear their footsteps as they walk from room to room above our heads, and I catch Yvette looking up at the ceiling with wonder. Maybe we'll get used to the *click-click-click* before long. The smell of smoke drifts down the stairs sometimes too, which isn't so nice, so I guess maybe Monsieur Coleman smokes. Some people smoke, but not my parents.

After supper, which tonight was chicken and stuffing, mashed potatoes with nice brown gravy, and carrots—not cabbage— Papa tells us a Ti-Jean story. He always smiles when he tells us these stories. So does Maman as she sits knitting by the table. Every time I look over my shoulder, she's watching me and she winks. Even though we hear the same stories again and again, they always sound different because Papa finds something new to add to them.

Today we hear the one about the three giant brothers who can tear trees out of the ground, roots and all. Birds fly down and peck at the giants' heads because they've been disturbed, so the giants wave their arms like windmills to chase the birds away. We all laugh because we've never heard that before, even Arthur, who is usually so serious. Ti-Jean sits in a tree and throws rocks at the giants. That way he tricks them into beating one another up with the trees they've pulled out until they're all lying in a giant heap on the ground. Then he tells the king that he took care of them himself. Ti-Jean always finds a way to make himself the hero.

Often, I wish that I could be as brave and clever as Ti-Jean.

Papa has flooded a skating rink in the backyard for us! It's already frozen because the weather has been so cold. So after Mass on Sunday morning, Bernard and I go out into the backyard to skate. Arthur can't be bothered. He'd rather stay inside and read another book by Jules Verne, who is his favorite author. And Yvette is complaining of a sore throat again. She always complains of a sore throat and sore ears, and she seems to cough a lot. Maman has made a mustard plaster for her back to draw out the sickness. Yvette cried when she had to put it on, which was no surprise. It burns but feels good, and Maman never leaves it on for very long.

Bernard and I bundle up to play outside. I wear a pair of Arthur's too-small breeches instead of my lisle stockings because it's so cold today. And a thick pair of wool socks. I also wear my older brother's *tuque*, which Maman knit, instead of my red felt hat from the United store. I even put on Arthur's jacket instead of my coat because he told me he didn't care. I wear Arthur's old skates stuffed with some newspaper. They feel a bit big but still work fine!

Outside, snowflakes sift down like flour from the sky as Bernard passes a horse ball hockey puck and I shoot it back with my hockey stick that Papa made. We skate back and forth on the rink pretending we are *les Canadiens de Montréal*. Bernard is Joe Benoit, and he tells me that I'm Toe Blake. We race each other, and I beat Bernard more times than he beats me. Papa is in the barn feeding his horses, and he checks on us now and then with a big smile on his face. He likes to watch us play hockey and skate on the rink that he built for us.

"Hey, *les p'tits gars*," I hear from the fence that runs alongside the road. When I look over, I can see Jeanine's pink face staring at me. She has a mean smile, and she's with her ugly friend Gilberte from school. "Are you having fun skating, little boys?" she shouts again.

At first, I'm not sure what she means, then it hits me. I'm dressed like a boy! Jeanine is calling me a boy! It makes me shaking mad! When Papa steps from the barn, scowling, the girls run away laughing. I don't care, I tell myself to help melt away my anger. I'm having fun skating in the backyard, and I know that when we go inside in a little while and hang our clothes to dry by the stove, Maman will have some hot tea with sugar ready for us, and maybe even some bread and molasses. And Jeanine will go home to a sick mother and a dirty house.

I turn around to have a backward skating race with Bernard. He always falls down on his bum whenever we skate backward, but I don't. As I cut smoothly across the ice on my skates, I catch sight of a face pressed against the frosty glass in the upstairs window of the bedroom that once was mine and Yvette's.

It's Carolyn Coleman, watching Bernard and me skate. I wonder if she has a pair of skates too, and if she might like to come out and join us on the ice rink. But just as I wave, her face disappears, leaving behind a patch of fog on the window.

8

Store-bought Cookies

On Monday, Jeanine Bonenfant doesn't come to school. I'm so glad because I know that today I don't have to worry about being teased by her in the schoolyard. Or about getting my face washed with snow on the way home for doing absolutely nothing wrong. Or getting slapped in the face or punched in the stomach again, which still hurts when I think about it. None of the Bonenfant children are here today, I notice at recess, and usually at least a couple of them turn up at school, except the oldest sister, who never comes at all. Sister Madeleine seems more content whenever Jeanine misses school. Today, nobody gets the strap, and she doesn't yell once.

After school, Georgette invites me to come to her house to play with her baby dolls. She has such nice ones, with pretty white bonnets and fancy nightgowns. She even has a Marie Dionne Quintuplet doll, which I'm not allowed to play with. It sits safely up on a shelf, dressed in a pretty blue robe, which is Marie's color. Georgette is fascinated with the Dionnes. She says she wishes she could be one of them instead of herself, Georgette Blondin, so she could have everything she ever wanted and wouldn't have to live in a house with parents who fight all the time. When I tell her that it would feel like living in a zoo, she just laughs at me.

All of Georgette's dolls have cloth bodies like my doll, and they don't have real hair, either, but they're much prettier than mine, and newer as well. And they have a whole wardrobe, so we can change their clothes. She always lets me play with the one that has blue eyes and long eyelashes and yellow hair. I wish I looked like that instead of my brown eyes and messy hair that never looks the same from one day to the next.

"And look at her cute little nose," I tell Georgette as I touch the tiny button. "I wish I had a nose like that instead of this ugly thing."

Georgette begins to laugh, and I grimace at her.

"Don't laugh, Georgette! How would you feel if you had a nose like mine?"

"I'm not laughing about your nose," she tells me, giggling. "I'm laughing because you'd look silly with a teeny nose like that one! Your nose is just fine, Aline. Mine is too wide, see," she says, pointing at the tip of it. "It's a big round ball. I don't like it."

"I wish we could trade," I tell her, and we both laugh.

"So, what do you want *le père Noël* to bring you this

Christmas?" Georgette asks, bouncing up and down on her bright store-bought bedspread with the pink and yellow rosebuds. "I'd like a new doll, a nurse doll, because when I grow up I want to be a nurse. I'd like some new paper dolls too. And a book. And my little brother wants Tinkertoys. And a toy fire truck. We're going to look at the toys in Ogilvy's soon. Are you? The store is so pretty in December, with all the bright lights and decorations."

I have never been to Ogilvy's. Sometimes, if we're lucky, Maman orders us brand new things from the Eaton's catalog. And a lot of the time, Maman buys clothes for us at a store called The Neighbourhood, on Wellington. Used clothes, not new ones. I always worry that people will know. I'm glad we must all wear black dresses with pleats, white collars, and cuffs to school. This way, nobody can see my Neighbourhood clothes, the ones I wear at home.

I sit quietly for a moment and pretend to comfort the baby doll on my shoulder. How do I tell Georgette that le père Noël hasn't brought any new toys to our house for a couple of years now? Papa has made us presents for Christmas, like the little crib and dresser for our dolls, the old ones we got a long time ago. And wooden toys for the boys. And our double-sided Parcheesi and checkerboard. And Maman knits things for us; once she even knitted some little coats for our dolls when she had yarn to spare, but that was a long time ago too. I would love a book, but I don't dare ask for one. I'm sure there's no money for books. Thank goodness for the Carnegie Library, so close by.

"Oh, I'm sure I'll be getting a new doll this Christmas too," I tell Georgette in a merry voice, even though I'm telling a lie. "One with real hair and beautiful clothes," I add, making it even worse for myself. "And two books." What's one more lie, after all? I hope my guardian angel and God won't be too disappointed in me.

"What books do you want?" Georgette asks, and I'm stumped for a moment. What should I tell her? The only books I read are the Delly books that I get from the library. And I can't think of any English book titles. Well, maybe *Black Beauty* or *Little Women*.

Before I can answer, though, I hear some loud voices coming from downstairs. It sounds as if Georgette's papa has just come home from work. There's a lot of clattering and banging from the kitchen. And Georgette's mother's voice is high and shrill when she asks, "What do you think you're doing, Henri? What's the matter with you?" Then she says *merde*! A swear word! That's when I hear a great scary crash, like dishes breaking, and a loud shout from Georgette's papa. I jump. Georgette's eyes grow wide and she cringes. There are footsteps running up the stairs now, and Georgette's younger brother, Jean, peeks around the half-open door.

"Papa has been drinking again," he tells his sister. "And now he's eating the chicken."

"Oh no," Georgette says, scowling. "And now Maman is mad at him again."

Jean nods, then disappears. We hear his bedroom door slam.

I frown. "Drinking what?" I ask her, and she starts laughing.

"Booze," she says. "Beer and whiskey, just like all the fathers around here. He wastes our money on it. You know how they like to stop for a drink after work? À *la taverne*."

"Not my father," I tell her. "He doesn't drink that stuff. He drinks lots of tea, though."

"Huh," Georgette says, frowning like she doesn't believe me. "That seems strange. We don't like it when our papa comes home drunk from the tavern. He acts stupid and talks too loud and yells at Maman, and she yells back at him. And then he eats like a big pig and doesn't leave enough meat for the rest of us. And doesn't even care."

"That's terrible." So terrible that my throat has tightened up.

She nods at me. "I know. It scares me," she says. "And sometimes when he does that, Maman pulls his hair and throws forks and spoons and even cups and plates at him, but never knives. That scares me too. Maybe you should go now, Aline."

"But I'm afraid to leave. I don't want to go past him in the kitchen," I tell her.

My winter clothes and boots and schoolbag are at the back door, where we came in and sat down to eat store-bought cookies and drink milk at the table. I couldn't believe that she was allowed to climb up in the cupboard and take the cookies without asking. We can never do that in our house, but I know where Maman hides the raisins and dates in her dining room armoire. I also know how to make it look as if none are missing. Right now, though, I just want to get out of this house fast, in case Madame Blondin throws something else at Monsieur Blondin.

"Don't worry, Aline. Wait by the front door. I'll get your things and bring them to you."

We creep down the stairway, and as Georgette hurries along the hall to the kitchen, I take a quick peek over my shoulder. I can see her papa sitting at the table. He has a whole chicken on a plate in front of him, and he's tearing a chicken leg with his greasy hands. Georgette's maman sits in a chair at the table, smoking a cigarette. Neither one is talking. I see her blow a puff of smoke right into her husband's face, and he doesn't even look up from his food. I can't begin to imagine being rich enough to eat a whole chicken by yourself!

After I get dressed quickly, I thank Georgette for the cookies and milk, and for letting me play with her dolls. Then I run all the way home in the almost dark. I can see people through their windows, in yellow lamplight that spills onto the snow, walking around in their houses or eating their supper at the table. I can't wait to get home, where my papa isn't a drunk and shares supper with all of us each and every day.

Christmas is getting closer. We know when we discover that Maman has strung up the red accordion bells across the kitchen by the time we get home one day after school later that week. And in a corner against the wall, on a table that once was in the living room, Bernard has begun to set up the manger scene of Bethlehem and the *crèche* where the Baby Jesus was born. He always starts in December when Advent begins, and it takes him a few days. First, he lays down a cloth painted in shades of brown and gray, which is the ground. Then he sets up a complete town of Bethlehem that he built himself. Next, he arranges all the clay figurines—the Holy Family, the shepherds and kings, the angels, and all the animals—that he bought at the five-and-dime and painted all by himself. He won't let anyone help him. He's even made palm trees somehow, with wood shavings as fronds. One year, Father Louis came over from the church and blessed it for us, so it's very special. I like to sit and stare at the scene because it looks so alive. And it means Christmas.

We never have a Christmas tree like everyone else does. But we do have a Christmas fruit bowl, for the oranges that we get to have once a year, and that bowl means Christmas too. It's the color of ivory, made of bone china, Maman tells us every year, and it once belonged to her grand-maman. It's "Hand-painted," it says on the back in English, with bright red and green sprigs of holly and a thin gold line around the rim. And it's "Made in England." *Just like Carolyn Coleman*, I can't help but think.

At the start of December each year, Maman steps onto the footstool and lifts the bowl carefully from a high shelf in the cupboard. She places it right in the middle of the kitchen table, on a lace doily. Then, like a miracle, the week before Christmas six oranges appear, one for each of us. But we have to wait until Christmas to eat them. That doesn't stop us from staring at them, though, and touching them and smelling them and looking forward to that sweet burst of juiciness in our mouths.

"Christmas is coming, Maman. Is it almost time to bring the fruit bowl out for the oranges?" I ask her after supper that night as I sit there admiring the red bells.

"Soon," Maman tells me, then quickly looks away. "You'll just have to wait a little bit longer, Aline," she adds with her back turned.

I stare at the sturdy back of her. She's wearing her blue housedress, and she's busy at the kitchen counter like she always is. Maman seems to be very patient all the time, with cooking, with doing laundry, with caring for her four young children, and even her barn cats. With having English tenants sleeping in her upstairs rooms. And with waiting for what will happen next in the war and trying not to worry about it too much.

She's always good at waiting. But I don't like waiting a little bit longer for anything. I don't like it one little bit.

9

Maroon Crape

First thing on Thursday morning, Sister Madeleine says she has an important announcement to make to the class. She tells us this in a very solemn voice, so I know it must be very important. She takes a deep breath and looks at all of us with sad eyes.

"Something terrible has happened," she says, and my heart twists in my chest. "Jeanine Bonenfant's mother has died. Just yesterday. That's why Jeanine hasn't been at school this week. Let's all say some prayers for Madame Bonenfant's soul, that Our Lord will meet her in heaven, and for Jeanine, her papa, and her brothers and sisters."

We all bow our heads. Together we recite three Hail Marys and the Our Father. I feel sick inside. *What must it be like for your mother to die?* I wonder. Why did God have to let her mother die? Is it maybe because Jeanine did bad things, like steal from her mother's purse and beat me up? Will my mother die because I stole money from her purse and never told? Does God punish you for sinning? Now I feel sicker and silently ask my guardian angel for help: *Angel of God, my guardian dear, to whom God's love entrusts me here, ever this day be at my side, to light and guard, to rule and guide. Amen.*

Will that help me at all? Now I'm not so sure anymore.

Sister Madeleine tells us that we should go to Jeanine's house to pay our respects to her family. Her mother will be there, in a casket in the living room for two days, and we can go any time because her family will sit up with Madame Bonenfant the whole time. And then we begin our lessons, but it's impossible for me to think today when I know that Jeanine's mother is lying dead in her living room.

There will be a maroon crape on their front door. That's how we know that there is someone dead inside a house. Once, on the way home from school, we passed a house with a crape on the door. My friend Thérèse told me and Lucille that she was going inside because she knew the person who died, the mother of a family whose children she looked after now and then. She said we could come along, but we were afraid, so we waited outside. Soon Thérèse came out wiping tears from her eyes, but she had a raisin bun in her hand and let us each have a bite.

After school that day, I sit quietly at the kitchen table. Maman sets a pet de sœur in front of me, knowing how much I love the little pastries filled with brown sugar and butter. I sit there just staring at it, though, not even hungry enough to take a bite. Maman wipes her hands on a tea towel and pulls a chair up beside me.

"What's wrong, Aline?" she asks, touching my arm. Her bright green eyes stare into mine from behind her glasses. Maman always knows when something is wrong.

"Madame Bonenfant died. She's the mother of Jeanine, a girl in my class who lives in Mechanicsville," I murmur.

"Oui, ma belle, Monsieur Nadeau told me today when he delivered the bread."

Already! And I'm sure he must have told everyone in the neighborhood that we have English Protestant tenants living in our house now and that they're buying bread and desserts from him. Maman never buys our desserts!

"I know of the Bonenfant family. I used to see Madame at the market and rummage sales before she got sick," Maman continues. "They have a lot of children, don't they? Poor woman. She was sick for a long time. Would you like to go and visit Jeanine?"

"Sister Madeleine said that we should," I tell my mother. Then I look down at the table. "Are you going to die soon too, Maman? Why did God let Jeanine's mother die when she had all those children to care for? And who will care for them now?"

Maman has a small smile on her face when I look up.

"First of all, Aline, we are all going to die someday. And second, I have no plans to die anytime soon. I have too much to do here on earth right now. I'm not nearly ready to go up and fly around with the angels in heaven." Now she's really smiling, and it makes me smile too. "Jeanine has an older sister, doesn't she? I'm sure her sister will be able to help out at home now that their maman has gone to heaven."

"But what if you get sick?" I ask her.

Maman shrugs. "Maybe I will. But then I'll get better. I told you, Aline. I'm too busy to get sick." She makes small, gentle circles on my back. "Tomorrow, after school, we will go to Jeanine's house and say a prayer for her mother, and we will tell her family that we're sorry, okay?"

I nod even though I'd rather be shaking my head. Then I bite into the warm pastry.

✱

On Friday, though, Maman can't come with me after all. Yvette is still sick and has a fever. She hasn't gone to school for most of the week, and she coughs most of the night, which makes it hard for us all to sleep in the living room. One night Arthur even threw his pillow at her and told her to cover her face when she coughs or we'll all get sick.

"But how can I go there alone?" I beg my mother for an answer. "I don't want to go there alone, Maman. I'm afraid to. Can't you come with me, please?"

"Yvette is too sick," Maman explains. When we hear Yvette coughing from the living room, our heads turn toward the painful sound. "The doctor came today and told me that she must have her tonsils taken out as soon as she feels a bit better. Don't tell her yet, though. I don't want her to be upset."

I heave a huge sigh. "Why did God have to create us with silly things like tonsils that we don't even need, anyway?"

"Maybe God is more like his people on earth than we know," Maman tells me. "Maybe even He can make mistakes sometimes."

My eyes fly wide open with alarm, and I gasp. How can my mother dare to say such things? "But Sister says Jesus was perfect," I argue. "And he's the Son of God."

Maman's eyes grow narrow. "Can someone who is human be perfect? I wonder," she says. "And even though Christ was human and divine, maybe He made some mistakes too. We don't know everything that happened to Him while He was on earth, do we?"

I gasp again. Surely she doesn't believe what she just said. She turns around and starts wiping the counter in big, fast circles.

"Now get ready to go, Aline," she tells me in a tight voice. "You'll be fine. And there will be other classmates there, I'm sure, if Sister told you to go. Pretend you're brave like our friend Ti-Jean, ma belle."

I don't think I can ever be that brave, but I'll try my best. Before I pull on all my winter clothes, though, I slip into the living room, where Yvette and I keep our dolls and furniture in the corner beside our bed. I peek at Yvette, lying there with her hair all matted and her face all red. Poor Yvette. I'm glad it's her and not me who is sick, though.

I quietly slide open the bottom drawer of the doll dresser. There's a space under that drawer where I've hidden the leftover candy from the money I stole. I still feel awful when I think about it, but not as much as before. I take out two peppermints, white with red stripes. I'll suck on one of them for courage while I walk across the railroad tracks to Mechanicsville and Jeanine's house. I'll suck on the other one while I walk home, to cheer me up after all the sadness.

In the kitchen, I pull on my boots, coat, hat, and mittens, then slip out the back door without even saying good-bye to Maman. When I pass the kitchen window, though, I can see her watching me.

✱

As soon as I've crossed Scott Street and get near the end of Hinchey Avenue, I know I'm getting close. That's when I start walking more slowly.

Already the darkness is settling in as the sun gets lower, and my long blue shadow walks beside me like a giant on the snowy road. It's grown colder, so my nostrils stick together and the snow scrunches under my boots. But I'm still sucking on my peppermint, and it's getting smaller and smaller. I tell myself that I won't step through Jeanine's door until it's all melted away by itself. I will not crunch it with my teeth, which means I have to slow down a lot because I'm almost there. And I don't want to be almost there yet.

When I turn the next corner, though, I feel a sudden burst of courage. Ahead of me, I spot my school friend Thérèse in her red coat and with her, two taller figures dark against the snow. Two Sisters, who walk so slowly it seems they're floating along the road. I know where they're going. To Jeanine's house. And I also know that it must be Sister Madeleine, my teacher, and Sister Marie, the principal, walking with Thérèse, so I hurry to catch up.

There are more people coming from the other direction now too, which fills me with even more courage. They're going to Jeanine Bonenfant's house for a look at her dead mother lying in the living room in a casket. I wonder if, like me, hardly anyone ever talked to her when she was alive, or even knew what she looked like. But everyone talked about her because she had so many children who brought bugs to school in their hair and sometimes had bruises and wore dirty, smelly clothes. And she had a mean drunk for a husband. And she never got out of bed for the past year. And I said bad things about Madame Bonenfant to Jeanine, and it makes me feel bad in my heart.

And now we're going to pray for her because she's dead.

10

Peppermint Candy

I reach the front of the Bonenfant house just as the last of the peppermint candy is gone, and my mouth still tingles from the sweet, minty taste. On the front door is a maroon crape. Nobody says a word as we climb the crooked front steps. The whole house seems crooked, and the paint is peeling on the wood like when I get a sunburn on my nose. Some of the window panes are cracked, and there is junk piled up on the porch. It looks dirty and messy like Jeanine, who always has dirty fingernails and dark streaks on her neck and hair that's never brushed.

Inside it's even worse, and it smells bad too. All the children are gathered around on chairs in the living room, and the room is dim because the curtains are almost shut and it's getting darker outside. Some of the older children cry, while younger ones poke one another and make faces. And Jeanine's older sister, Jacqueline, is holding a crying, squirming baby.

There is only one lamp, not very bright, in a corner. The couch is old, with rips and some springs popping out. The floor is dirty and wet from people's boots. Some visitors in the small, stuffy room have rosaries in their hands and mutter to themselves, eyes closed. And up against the wall is the casket, with a kneeler in front of it, like in church. And in it is something that is supposed to be Jeanine Bonenfant's mother but looks like a big waxy doll.

In a chair beside the casket sits Monsieur Bonenfant. His face is like stone, and he's staring straight ahead. I wonder why he isn't crying when his wife is dead. I've never seen my own papa cry. But I know he would if our maman died. I catch sight of Jeanine standing in a corner. She's wearing her school uniform still, like I am. Even though she wasn't at school today. It makes me wonder if she has any other "decent" clothes. Maman makes sure that we always have some decent clothes, even if they come from The Neighbourhood store.

Someone nudges me from behind, and I look up into Sister Madeleine's kind face.

"Go over to the casket now, girls, then kneel down and say a prayer," she whispers to Thérèse and me.

We walk a few slow steps to the kneeler, where a man and woman kneel with their heads bowed, praying. When they stand and step aside, Thérèse and I kneel in their places and the nuns stand behind us. Beside me, I hear a soft cough from Thérèse and when I take a quick sideways look, her face is screwed up, then she buries her nose in her hand.

It feels as if there is a giant lump in my throat, and I can't even swallow. My face is less than two feet away from Madame Bonenfant's face, and it's a terribly awful sight. There is pink powder on her pale cheeks, her lips seem stretched to the side, and her brown hair looks like doll hair. Her stiff hands are folded and hold a rosary. They don't look real, either, more like candle wax. Nothing looks real, maybe because she *isn't* anymore.

Madame's Bonenfant's soul has gone to heaven to be with Our Lord, and only her rigid, hard body is left behind. Once I find the courage to look, I can't tear my eyes away, and it's so terrible and awful that I haven't even said a prayer yet. Instead, I stare at Jeanine's mother's eyes to see if they're moving under the closed lids. Oh, and I'm so afraid that maybe they'll fly open and stare back and make me scream. Then I feel something poke into my back and I jump.

When I look up, Sister Marie is staring down at me. When I stand up, she hooks her arm through mine and leads me away, and I realize that Thérèse isn't even beside me anymore. When I reach the front doorway again, Jeanine is standing there. There is no trace of her usual half-smirk, her narrow threatening eyes, or her blabbering rubbery mouth that likes to stick its tongue out at everyone in the world. For the first time ever, her face looks completely blank and harmless. She reaches out a hand and shakes mine, Thérèse's, and the nuns'.

"*Merci*," she says. "Thank you for coming."

And one tear slides slowly down her cheek. That's when my tears come, at the thought of losing Maman. How will she live without her maman? As the nuns try to steer us back out into the cold darkness, I grope for something to say, but the words won't come. Just as I'm about to step through the doorway, I shove my hand into my pocket and pull out the peppermint candy. I grab Jeanine's hand and push the candy into it, just as Sister pushes me out the door. For an instant, I catch sight of Jeanine's face as she's closing the door. It almost looks as if she might be smiling, just a little. Then she presses her hand flat against the window pane in what almost looks like a wave.

I run all the way home alone through the dark as tears soak my face and turn to frost. As soon as I burst through the door, I go right over in my snowy boots and wrap my arms around Maman, who stands by the stove.

"You were a very brave girl today, Aline," she whispers over my head.

I sob into her chest, and her gentle hand strokes my hair. Slowly, slowly, I begin to feel like myself again. Safe and warm in my kitchen, just in time for supper.

The funeral is on Saturday, but Maman says I don't have to go, that I've been brave enough this week. She goes to the church, along with another mother on the street. I stand in the window and watch her walking off through the applesauce slush in the direction of Saint-François d'Assise in her gray tweed coat, black felt church hat, and sturdy rubber boots, her black purse hooked over her arm. Then a while later the hearse carrying Jeanine's mother glides slowly along our street toward the church, followed by a procession of somber men dressed in black, the neighborhood men who are paying their respects to the Bonenfant family. Papa and Arthur join the procession as it passes, and I stay home with Bernard and Yvette.

Yvette is still not well, but I don't want to tell her what will happen next week when she has to get her tonsils taken out. I give her a cup of warm chicken broth that Maman had prepared and try to help her catch up on some of her homework while sitting on the edge of the bed beside her. But I can tell she's not in the mood, and her face is flushed, and she sounds like she's growling when she talks. Maman says that her tonsils are like a couple of big red strawberries at the back of her throat. I ask her to open her mouth so I can take a look inside, and it's true. I can barely see her throat hole because of the big red lumps plugging up where she swallows. They look as fiery as her face.

Yvette tells me in a hoarse voice that she doesn't want to do her schoolwork right now and would rather play a game. So I fetch the wooden game board from the kitchen cupboard, and we play a game of Parcheesi on the bed. I let Yvette win three times, but soon I can see that my sister is tired. She settles back on her pillow and her eyes slowly close.

Bernard is playing hockey out on the street with some friends, but I have to stay inside with Yvette. Musical notes drift from the radio upstairs. I recognize the voice of Bing Crosby singing "White Christmas." Georgette has played it for me on her phonograph a few times. I stand in the hallway to listen for a moment. It's the most popular Christmas song on the radio right now. And then I hear Madame Coleman's voice joining in. It sounds like Bing is upstairs singing with her! I don't know all of the English words, but I recognize some of them, like *children* and *sleigh bells* and *snow*. I like the word *glisten*, so I say it over and over again. It sounds like a shiny word to me. Like our French word *scintiller*. I wish we had a phonograph like Georgette's family so we could buy Bing's record and listen to it over and over again too.

I'm about to head for Papa's rocking chair to curl up and read from my Delly book that I borrowed from the French section of the Carnegie Library last week when I hear a door open upstairs. Then the click of heels on the steps. In the hallway where I'm standing, I look up. And see her looking down at me. Carolyn Coleman.

"What are you doing down there, little girl?" she asks me.

"I am not a little girl," I tell her in my broken English, and she grins.

"You talk funny," she says with a giggle.

"*Toi aussi*," I tell her.

Carolyn frowns. "What did you just say?" she asks me, and I grin back at her.

"You too," I tell her in English, and she giggles again.

"Toi aussi," she tries to say in French but gets it wrong. That makes me giggle.

I realize she's holding something in her hand. It's an orange, the biggest one I've ever seen. And it's already peeled. How can she have an orange already when it isn't even Christmas yet? We only have them at Christmas, on the table in the bone china fruit bowl that Maman brings down from the shelf every December. Carolyn sees me staring at the orange.

"You want some? We have plenty of them."

I'm speechless. All I can do is nod. She breaks the orange in half and hands it to me through the banister rails, and I can't believe my eyes. There's juice dripping from her fingers, and as soon as the orange is in my hand, juice drips from mine too. This is the juiciest orange I've ever seen in my whole life.

"Merci," I murmur breathlessly, and she tips her head.

"What?" Carolyn asks.

"Oh, tank you," I tell her in my broken English, after realizing I spoke in French.

Carolyn laughs again, then runs *clickety-clack* back up the stairs. I head straight for the rocking chair with my prize. There I sit and rock slowly, crush each slice of orange in my back teeth, and let the juice run down my throat. I should save this slice for poor sick Yvette because maybe it would help her feel better. But I swallow it, instead. I keep telling myself, after each slice, that I will save the rest for my family. But then I eat just one more until there is only one left, and that's not nearly enough to share with six people, so I swallow that one too.

"You are a greedy girl today," my guardian angel whispers into my ear. And in my other ear, I'm sure I can hear the devil laughing at both of us.

11

Too Many Pieces to Fix

Once, when I was in Grade 5, our teacher gave us a description to write. We had to go home and describe our house, the outside and the inside, room by room. After supper, when I sat at the kitchen table and began my homework, Papa asked what I was working at. When I explained, his face grew solemn and he took the pencil out of my hand.

"It's nobody's business what the inside of our house looks like," Papa told me. "You can tell your teacher I said that if you want to."

I couldn't tell my teacher that. Instead, I told her I forgot to do my homework, and she gave me an E. And a long lecture about being irresponsible, which I didn't listen to.

On Monday morning, it happens again. Sister gives us a scrapbook project. We are to cut out pictures of different sorts of vegetables and fruits from magazines and from tin-can labels.

It's about the sort of foods that people eat every day, what they have in their cupboards and iceboxes. We can work on it over the Christmas holidays. As she stands at the front of the class explaining, I look around in desperation, knowing that I can't do this project, either.

We don't have any cans with labels in our house. We have glass jars in the cellar with wild crabapples in sweet syrup that Maman stewed in the fall. We have jars of strawberry and raspberry jam made from fruit my sister and I spent hours picking in the hot sun at Tunney's Pasture. The cans in our cupboard are all dented and they have no labels. Maman doesn't know what's inside of them, either. She gets them from the market for pennies and takes a chance on what's inside. Sometimes it's a nice surprise, like the cherries she used in a pie once. Other times it's not so nice, like the yucky clams we had to eat in the soup she made from them.

We don't have any magazines in our house, either. We only have *Le Droit*, the newspaper that comes every day, and there are no pictures of food in it. And after Maman, Papa, and Arthur read it, Maman puts it in the bathroom so we can wipe ourselves because toilet paper is too expensive. And we have the Eaton's catalog that comes in the mail, with beautiful new clothes and all sorts of other things Yvette and I love to look at, but not the kind of food pictures I need for this project. But maybe there's somebody who can help me with today's problem.

I glance toward Georgette's desk. The Blondins have tin cans in their cupboard, I know it for certain. And they have magazines too. Georgette even has them in her bedroom. Maybe she can get some pictures for me so I can do the scrapbook project. But Georgette hasn't come to school today. That seems very strange because Georgette never misses school and always does her homework and gets good marks like me. Where could she be? I decide that I'll stop at her house after school to ask if I can have some of her can labels and pictures from her magazines.

Jeanine is at school today, though. The funeral for her maman was on Saturday, and last Friday when I went to her house she was crying. Not today, though. She came to school late as usual, slammed the door, and shuffled to her desk in her wet boots. Today, Sister didn't say a word, but her face turned red and she broke a piece of chalk when she was writing on the blackboard. And Jeanine sat at her desk smirking. When I turned around to look at her, to see if she might wave at me again, her eyes were narrow and she looked the other way. I don't think I'll ever be a friend of hers, and I don't even think that I want to be one.

At recess, I play with Lucille and Thérèse, since Georgette is away. I wonder if she's sick, like so many other girls are right now, with sore throats and colds, like Yvette. As the three of us roll a big ball for the head of the snowman that we're building, I glance toward the corner of the schoolyard where Jeanine and Gilberte and the other big dumb girls usually play in the snow. Today, though, Jeanine isn't with them.

"Big dumb Jeanine is quieter today," Thérèse says, snickering. "You should have seen inside her house, Lucille. It was such a dirty mess. And it smelled so bad in there! Pew!" She makes a face and pinches her nose.

"Be quiet," I tell her. "That's not nice, Thérèse. Especially since her mother just died!"

Thérèse just sticks out her tongue at me.

I see Jeanine walking by herself at the edge of the schoolyard with a stick in her hand that she's clattering along the fence. Just walking slowly and staring straight ahead. I can't help but wonder if maybe she's thinking about her maman. I know I would be if I were her, if my maman had just died. Then, for the rest of the morning, she stays very quiet at her desk.

I prayed to my favorite saint, Sainte Thérèse, for Jeanine and her family when I was in church on Sunday. I hope she and Our Lord were listening. Before communion, I also asked forgiveness for eating the orange.

When I get home for lunch, Maman serves me vegetable soup with macaroni in it. Today, she made cheese sandwiches for the boys, she explains, because they wanted to eat their lunch at school. Then she sits down across from me at the table, looking serious.

"Yvette's fever is gone now, and she's feeling better. But she still needs to have her tonsils taken out, the doctor said, so she won't keep getting sick all the time. Tomorrow is the day. Don't tell her that, okay?" Maman says, patting my hand. "I don't want her to worry too much about it."

"Poor Yvette! I won't tell her Maman. Will it hurt very much?" I can't even imagine!

"Yes, but the doctor will give her some special medicine, so she will be asleep when he does it." Then Maman pauses and her face seems to flicker like a candle for a moment. "Was Georgette Blondin at school today?"

"No, she wasn't. But how did you know?"

Maman closes her eyes and shakes her head.

"When Monsieur Nadeau stopped by, he told me that their house is vacant. He tried to deliver their bread today, but nobody was there. He found out from a neighbor that Monsieur Blondin lost his delivery job and has just disappeared. Nobody knows where he went. And that Madame Blondin took Georgette and Jean to Montreal to live with her maman." She shakes her head once again and sighs. "So very sad for your poor friend, Aline."

I can't believe what I'm hearing. "But what about all of their beautiful things? What about their phonograph and Georgette's beautiful dolls and all the good food in their cupboards and their nice furniture?"

"I don't know, ma belle. Maybe they took some of it, or maybe they left it behind or sold it." She clucks her tongue. "I'm so glad we have our own house," she murmurs.

"You mean that wasn't their own house?" I ask my mother.

"No, they were renting it, like so many of the other families around here," Maman explains. "Sometimes when people rent their houses, they have more money for lots of other things. We don't because we want to pay for our house, so we can own it someday. We save every penny that we can to give back to the bank because the bank let us borrow some money to build our house. So we can't have a lot of special things like some other people can."

I almost choke on a spoonful of soup just thinking of the ten cents that I took from my mother's purse. No wonder she never has any money to spare for Sister's charity box. But I took it from her purse and when the box was gone, I didn't give the money back. I went to the store and bought candy and shared it with Lucille. And we ate like little pigs, then she threw up all over her boots. And some of that candy is still hidden in the space under the doll dresser drawer. I'm afraid it won't even taste sweet in my mouth anymore because it's almost like stolen candy. I wish I could just throw it all away, but I don't know where and that would be wasting.

Maman looks very sad. "And this Christmas, well, there won't be much for you and Yvette and your brothers. I'm afraid that le père Noël might not be able to stop here. It's been a very hard year for everyone." She sits and watches me. "Do you understand?"

"Are we very, very poor, Maman?" I ask because I want to hear her say it herself. I want to understand how poor we are.

Maman sits and stares at me for a moment, then looks down at her rough hands. We all have chapped hands in winter but no cream. Maman tells us to pee on them to help them heal. It stings, but it works.

"Do you ever feel hungry, Aline?" Maman asks me. "Do you always get enough meat and potatoes at suppertime? Is there always a pot of soup on the stove for your lunch and hot porridge for your breakfast? And fresh eggs? And chickens?"

I nod. There's always food, even if it's pork fat from the frying pan spread on bread. Which is a treat we all fight over, but when I told Georgette about it, she made a yucky face and said that her mother throws that stuff away. Maman doesn't waste a crumb. And sometimes, like on wash day, we have cornflakes for breakfast because it's faster for Maman than making porridge. And we always have good dessert, like tapioca and rice pudding and bread pudding and thumbprint jam cookies and raisin buns. And pies, always pies. Everything made by Maman, never bought from Monsieur Nadeau. Maman says that he delivers bread and desserts to our tenants upstairs.

"Bon," Maman says. "Are you warm enough in your bed at night and when you go outside every day? Do you have clean clothes to wear without any holes in them?"

I nod again. Sometimes my face gets cold, and sometimes my fingertips, but I don't really notice when I'm walking to school or playing outside. And there are plenty of warm wool blankets and quilts for our beds. And even though our clothes aren't always new ones ordered from Monsieur Eaton, they're always clean and tidy. Maman washes them every Monday. Sometimes I stir in the rag with the bluing tied inside of it that helps make the sheets whiter. Maman would never stand for gray sheets like the ones she sees on some of the other women's clotheslines on our street.

"Are you happy?" Maman asks. "Living here, in this house, with Papa and me, with your brothers and sister?"

I nod again. I'm not sure I've ever felt unhappy. I've felt angry at my brothers for teasing me sometimes, and at Jeanine Bonenfant for chasing me and punching me and throwing snow in my face. I know I've been jealous of some of the things that my friends have, and lately I've been a bit greedy. But most of the time, I know I'm happy. I remember Jeanine's face today. I don't think she's very happy. Maybe she never has been.

"Now, do you think we're very, very poor, Aline?" Maman asks, gently patting my arm. "Or do you think that maybe we're a little bit rich?"

I'm not sure. I do know that we're different. We're not like the rich ones with the nice clothes and the store-bought cookies and the pretty dolls and the money to give to charity. Neither are we like the Dionnes, who seem to have everything they could ever want—except for their parents. They have nurses and a doctor instead and live in a different house than their family. There are the princesses, Elizabeth and Margaret, who live in a palace in England with their parents, the king and queen. They have beautiful clothes and houses and lives. I wonder if they're happy, or if they know that they're rich.

We're not like the poor ones, either, who come to school smelling bad, with dirty and holey clothes, and have bugs crawling in their hair all the time instead of just a few times like us. The ones who swear and never do their schoolwork and have fathers who are drunks, though some of the rich ones have fathers like that too.

I'm still not sure what to say to Maman, so instead I just nod. Then I ask her a question.

"Maman, where's the pretty china fruit bowl? For the Christmas oranges. It's already December, and you haven't taken it down from the cupboard to put on the table yet."

Maman starts blinking quickly. She looks toward the cupboard, then back at the table and the empty spot in the center where she traditionally places the fruit bowl.

"I didn't want to tell you this." Maman touches her throat. "But now it's time. The other day, I climbed up on a chair to take down the fruit bowl. And Aline, I dropped it. It broke into too many pieces to fix, so I had to throw it away. I'm so sorry. Please don't tell the others until they notice, okay? And then when they ask me, I'll tell them too. It's not that important anyway, is it?"

"But I thought you loved that bowl, Maman," I whisper. "That's what you said once."

"But it's only a bowl, isn't it, Aline?" Maman murmurs. "Only a bowl."

I nod and blink back some tears that have filled my eyes. Maman pats my hand again and gets up to stir something on the stove while I sit there thinking as I quietly finish my soup.

I know what I have to do. I have to tell Sister Madeleine the truth about this scrapbook project. I have to confess that I won't be able to do it because we don't have cans with labels or magazines at our house like everyone else does. I only hope she'll understand.

12

Red Lollipop

On Tuesday, Maman gives us our lunch to take to school. This morning, Yvette is going to the hospital to have her tonsils out and will spend the night there. Tomorrow, Papa and Maman will go pick her up in the sled and bring her home. And she doesn't even know yet. That helps me forget about the broken fruit bowl that I'm not allowed to talk about. I feel so sorry for my sister, and so glad that after her operation today she'll finally start to feel better. She won't cough and groan and toss around in our bed all night long. She'll be able to sleep better, and so will the rest of us who sleep in the living room now. And pretty soon, she'll come back to school and be able to play with us again.

Maman always makes us sandwiches when we stay at school for lunch. Sometimes we get hard cheese on bread, which is very dry because Maman wraps it in brown paper. We don't have waxed paper like others do, so I always try to unwrap my sandwich on my lap in case someone notices in my class. Other times, maybe we'll get a bit of pork if there's enough, but it's mostly saved for Papa because he has to work so hard delivering wood with his horses and his sled.

When we were little, we used to like watching Henri and Billie, our two huge workhorses. We used to stand and look at them in their stalls and laugh when yellow piss streams poured out or steaming horse balls dropped to the floor. We liked to watch them play in the yard, chasing and nipping at each other, or rolling on their backs in the sand or snow. Papa would even give us rides on their broad backs sometimes and let us stroke their whiskers. But now I'm ashamed of them and hide under the hay when Papa drops us off at school because it must mean that we're poor. And even though Maman thinks that maybe we're a bit rich, I still duck down on the way to school Tuesday when I get a ride because Papa's going that way.

That doesn't stop me from hearing the snowballs smack the sled, though. And when I peek out through the slats, I can see Jeanine Bonenfant leering and laughing because she knows that I'm in here hiding. She must feel better now—she's acting like the old Jeanine again.

I don't get a chance to tell Sister that I can't do the Christmas scrapbook project because that morning is one of the worst ever for Sister Madeleine, and for the rest of us. Today, Jeanine is acting completely *folle*, completely crazy. She walks into class very late and makes too much noise, and she swears when Sister asks her to sit down. So that finally Sister has to do it. She has to give her the strap, even though she looks more miserable than Jeanine while she's doing it. And even worse, Jeanine just laughs in her face, which makes Sister smack even harder, which makes Jeanine laugh even harder, which makes Sister so furious that she drops the strap on her desk and stalks toward the classroom door.

That's when the awful thing happens. As she's passing the radiator where all our wet mittens and hats are drying, her veil catches on something. But she keeps on walking, and the radiator yanks her veil right off! And Sister Madeleine shrieks before fleeing through the door. We hear her hurrying footsteps in the hallway. Her veil is left behind, dangling from the rad.

There is complete silence in the classroom. We all know what we saw, and we also know that it was an awful sight. Because what we've always wondered, what we've always whispered and giggled about, we finally know for certain. Sister has no hair under her veil. Well, she has a little bit, but it's shorter than my brothers' hair. It's shorter than the bristles on my hairbrush. And very black. And it was a very scary thing to see. And I wonder if Sister will even come back to the classroom today, or ever. And after that, Jeanine just thumps back into her seat.

A few minutes later when I dare to peek over my shoulder,

Jeanine is slumped over her desk with her face buried in the crook of her arm. I think I can see her shoulders shaking a little, like what happens to me when I cry. We all murmur among ourselves because others have noticed that Jeanine is crying. We all stare in wonder. Then Sister Marie, the principal, swoops into the room, all flapping habit and rattling beads. She doesn't look at any of us, just crouches down and carefully plucks Sister Madeleine's veil from the radiator.

"Work quietly at your desks on some arithmetic," she tells us when she stands up, the veil folded neatly over her arm. We all nod.

Then she grabs Jeanine by the ear and pulls hard.

"Come with me," she commands, and Jeanine leaps out of her seat, her face all red and wet. Sister still has a hold of her ear and isn't letting go. And we hear "Ow, ow, ow," all the way down the hall. Then Sister's office door slamming shut. Then nothing.

After recess, Sister Madeleine comes back wearing her veil once more and acts as if nothing happened. And so do we because we know it's best for all of us to pretend that the awful thing never happened this morning. And we do our grammar and our social studies, have our lunch, and in the afternoon do more work, like science and arithmetic.

And all day long I wait to hear the too-big boots of Jeanine Bonenfant shuffle along through the hallway to our classroom. But on Tuesday she doesn't come back at all. And for the rest of the school day, and all the way home, I can't stop wondering about her.

Tuesday night, Yvette stays over in the hospital, all by herself. *Poor Yvette*, I think every time I awaken during the night and the spot beside me in bed is empty and cold. And every time, I say a little prayer that God will keep her safe and make her well again. Between Jeanine and my sister, it seems like I'm always worrying about something.

When I get home from school on Wednesday, Maman isn't in the kitchen, but there's a big pot of soup simmering on the stove. When I lift the lid, I see chicken boiling. I find my mother sitting on the bed with Yvette. My sister is bringing up some blood into a bowl. And crying nonstop. Maman pats her forehead with a damp cloth.

Maman says it will take some time for her to recover. *I'm so glad it's her and not me.* And I feel so bad for even thinking that! I would love to fetch a lollipop for Yvette from my hiding place in the little dresser, but Maman might see me and find out what I did. And I haven't even told Father Louis at confession yet.

Yvette can't eat anything, and all she does is sleep after she finishes being sick. Everyone in the house is quiet tonight. We can hear music playing on the radio upstairs where the Colemans live. But it's not very loud because Maman has told Madame Coleman about Yvette. When I hurry upstairs to use the toilet, the door to their kitchen is closed and behind it their voices are just murmurs.

Maman looks worried and keeps going to check on Yvette, putting a hand on her forehead and on her hot, red cheek. I know because I follow her every time and feel like there's a tight elastic band inside my chest that's about to snap.

"Will Yvette be able to have supper with us?" I ask with a cheerful voice. Yvette has always loved to eat but lately hasn't eaten much at all. Her face looks thinner than ever.

"Non, ma belle," Maman tells me with an almost-smile. "She can only drink for a couple of days, and then eat jello and custard. I will save her some chicken broth for when she wakes up, and then we'll try some boiled eggs or mashed potatoes later this week. I wish I knew how to cheer her up because she's feeling pretty miserable right now."

I nod. I think I know a way. And I think I'll try to make it happen.

After our supper, my brothers and I do our homework quietly at the kitchen table, and we don't even argue the way we usually do, fighting for the sharpest pencil or who gets to sit closest to the stove. When I look at my brothers' faces, I can tell that they're worried too. So is Papa, who offered up the rosary to Yvette's convalescence tonight, then asked us to say some extra prayers for our sister when we go to bed.

Maman makes a little nest for me that night on the floor in the living room because it's better not to sleep in bed beside Yvette tonight. I'm happy with this plan because what if my sister brings up some blood during the night? I help Maman put some quilts on the floor, and then lay my head on my pillow beside the bed. I listen as the house gets quiet and the lights are turned out in each room, and I can hear the whiffles and snores of everyone in my family; my brothers across the room, my parents in their dining room bedroom. And I can hear the sleepy murmurs and painful whines of my sister in the bed beside my nest. She isn't better yet, that I know.

That's when I crawl over to the little doll dresser on the floor in the corner, slide the bottom drawer out, and grope through the collection of candy in the dark until my hand lands on a lollipop.

The next morning, I move the lollipop from under my pillow to inside my blue mitten before anyone can notice. I plan on sneaking it to Yvette after breakfast. It's a red lollipop, and I'm glad because I know that's Yvette's favorite color. Before leaving for school, when I'm all bundled up, I go into the living room to say goodbye to my sister. For once she didn't cough all night, but she moaned a lot, and Maman kept checking on her.

I stand staring down at her in our bed. She looks sweaty and pale and small lying there underneath her comforter. I'd like to leave the lollipop with her right now, but she's still asleep, and if

I leave it on the bed beside her, Maman will notice it. And then I will have to tell her the truth about the dime I stole. I want to hand it to Yvette and tell her to keep it hidden under the covers and lick it when Maman isn't watching. And when she's finished, she can give me back the stick and I will throw it into the stove to burn up when Maman isn't looking.

But I don't have a chance because Yvette is asleep. So I'll have to carry the lollipop to school in my blue mitten, then wait until I get home to give it to my sister. I kiss her forehead lightly before I hurry outside for a ride in the sled on this frosty morning.

Today, Jeanine doesn't come to school. And Sister Madeleine is very quiet. She doesn't smile much, but she doesn't get upset with us at all, either, even if we aren't focusing on our work properly or are fidgeting too much in our seats. She keeps glancing toward the door as if she expects Jeanine to arrive at any moment. But it's hard to tell by the strange look on her face whether Sister is happy or sad when she never shows up that morning.

Then, as I get dressed to go outside for afternoon recess, Sister calls me up to the front of the class and asks me to wait a moment until everyone else has gone outside. I spot Thérèse waiting for me at the door, but I tell her to go ahead without me. Then I look at Sister.

Her light green eyes look troubled. She has a pretty face, with a nice nose and creamy- looking skin, and sometimes I wonder why she became a nun instead of a wife and mother. Why did she choose to wear a habit every day, with a wimple tight around her face, with a heavy veil hiding her closely shorn head of hair? Sometimes Father Louis comes over from the parish church and talks to us about our calling in life, says that the Sisters are always looking for young women to serve Our Lord. Maybe our brother Bernard wants to be a Christian Brother and walk around in a long black robe all day, but I never want to be a nun. I would never want to look like a crow for the rest of my life.

"Have you heard anything from Jeanine?" Sister asks me. "Have you spoken to her or seen her since yesterday?"

"Why would I hear from Jeanine Bonenfant, Sister, when we're not even friends?" I say. *When she always beats me up*, I think in my head.

"You're not friends?" Sister asks. "That isn't what Jeanine told Sister Marie yesterday morning in the office. She said that the two of you are friends."

"Friends? Us?" I wonder if I've heard correctly. "Why did she say that?"

Sister pauses, then looks at me with sadness in her eyes.

"I thought maybe you could tell me, Aline," she says.

"But I don't know why, Sister," I confess.

Sister looks very serious for a moment. She sighs and shakes her head. "Jeanine and her family are in a very difficult situation right now. They have been for quite a while. It helps to explain why she is always acting up in class. And now that her mother has passed away, it's become even worse. You understand this, don't you?"

I nod, even though I don't quite understand. As long as I've known Jeanine, she's been trouble—either making it or getting into it. Reckless, bold, and always bad, she's close friends with the devil and never the least bit sorry for anything she does. She's picked on me for two years now, ever since her family moved to Mechanicsville, and I don't know why.

And yesterday she told Sister Marie that I'm her friend. This doesn't make any sense to me. How could I ever be friends with a girl like her?

"Sister Marie and I are worried about her," Sister continues. "She needs somebody to talk to, but she won't open up to us. We asked if she wanted to talk to Father Louis, but she said no. We asked if she has any friends she could talk to, and she said maybe you, Aline."

"But she hates me." I spit out the word like there's bad-tasting medicine in my mouth.

"But you went to her house to pay your respects last week, along with Thérèse," Sister reminds me. "And you were the only classmates who went. You were the only students in the whole school who went. Not even the girls she plays with at recess went to visit her house."

"Because you said we should go. And I guess because I felt sorry for her because she doesn't have a mother anymore. I wanted to see her mother." I'm also pretty sure that Thérèse only went over to the Bonenfant house to snoop, so she could say even more bad things about Jeanine. But I don't tell Sister that.

Sister smiles. She's even prettier when she smiles. Then she pats my shoulder.

"That's what I thought," Sister says. "And I wonder if that's why she called you her friend. Because you went to her house."

"But just yesterday she threw a snowball at my papa's sled," I tell Sister.

"Jeanine is Jeanine," Sister says with a shrug. "And there's a good chance that she will never change. But that doesn't mean she isn't hurting inside. Or that she doesn't need a friend. Thank you for talking to me, Aline."

"Sister, there's one more thing," I say, because now I finally have a chance to tell her.

"What's that, Aline?" she asks. Her eyes are still kind-looking, her face gentle.

"Sister, I can't do the scrapbook project over Christmas," I murmur, afraid that someone else might overhear and realize how poor we are.

"And why is that?" Sister says, frowning now.

I'm almost too embarrassed to explain, but I do anyway.

"Because...well...we don't have any cans with labels or even any magazines at our house," I whisper.

Sister's frown melts away and her face turns soft again.

"Think nothing more of it," Sister says and places one hand

on my head. "You can go and catch up with your friends outside now. You still have a few more minutes to play."

I run out the door into the schoolyard without looking back, feeling ashamed about the confession I just made to Sister. Still, it's a relief that she didn't get mad at me. I play in the snow with the other girls, but keep glancing toward the corner where Jeanine usually plays. It looks half empty there without her too-strong body and her too-loud voice taking up space. And I can't get Jeanine Bonenfant out of my mind at school for the rest of the day.

13

Ice Cream

All day long I've had the red lollipop tucked inside my mitten: whenever I was playing outside at recess, all the way home for lunch and all the way back, and now all the way home again after school as I skip along with my arm hooked through my cousin Lucille's. It's getting a bit sticky. Even though the devil is sitting on my shoulder trying to tempt me to eat it, I resist. Yvette needs this candy far more than I do. I don't even tell Lucille about the lollipop.

The red lollipop helps me forget about Jeanine Bonenfant for the time being too, because I can't wait to get home and hand it to Yvette. I didn't mention to Thérèse what Sister told me at recess, and I don't tell Lucille on the way home, either. For once, I'm holding on to my very own secret inside my soul, but I can feel it scratching to get out. Like one of Maman's cats at the back door in the morning.

✳ III ✳

All these thoughts are murmuring in my head like sparrows in our lilac bush when Lucille stops dead on the road just before we round the corner onto Hinchey Avenue. When I turn to look at her, she's looking back at me funny.

"I know a secret," she says, then slaps her hand over her mouth as if the secret is about to fly out.

"No you don't," I tell Lucille. It's the best way to get her to tell me because my cousin is even worse at keeping secrets than I am.

"Yes I do," she says, stamping her boot in the snow. "And it's about my papa and yours."

I narrow my eyes at her. "What do you know? You have to tell me because we're cousins. We're family, even if our fathers don't talk to each other."

She leans forward and whispers to me as if someone might be listening. "And now I know why." She steps back and smiles slyly.

"I don't believe you, Lucille," I tell her. "How could you find something out when nobody ever talks about it?"

"Because I heard my parents arguing when they thought I was asleep in my room last night," Lucille tells me. "I told Maman about Yvette being so sick. And she wanted to make some ice cream for her, to help her get better. We have an ice-cream churn, and Maman made my two little brothers ice cream when they had their tonsils out. But my papa told her not to do it!"

I know Lucille's family has a hand-crank ice-cream machine. In the summer, she brags about it all the time. On hot days, I see her and her brothers eating ice cream on their front porch. It makes me very jealous, but I know it's a sin to "covet thy neighbor's goods." Sometimes in winter Maman tries to make ice cream by setting a bowl of vanilla and cream outside in the snow. It doesn't ever work out very well; it's too watery but tastes good anyway.

I place my hands on Lucille's shoulders and stare straight into her eyes.

"Tell me your secret right now. Tell me every single thing you heard. I'm not letting you go home until you do. Understand?"

Lucille's eyes open wide. She thinks I'm mad at her, when I'm really not. I'm just desperate to find out her secret.

"*Bon*," she says. "I'll tell you, Aline, but you can't tell anyone else. Promise?"

"Of course. I can keep a secret. You know that, Lucille. I'm good at it."

"Well, I heard my maman say to my papa that he should try to make peace with your father, even if…" She draws in a huge breath, and I feel like shaking her to make her hurry up and finish, "'Jacques never forgave his mother for taking you in when you were a baby, and he never will. Even if Emilie wants him to.' That's exactly what my mother said to him."

Jacques is my papa's name, Emilie is my maman's, and I can't believe what I'm hearing.

"You're making that up!" I yell into my cousin's face. "You're telling a lie about our fathers, and now you have to go to confession!"

When Lucille's eyes fill with tears, I know that I'm wrong and that she's telling the truth. My cousin never tells lies. She knows that lying is a sin.

"It's really and truly true?" I whisper, and she nods and brushes away her tears. The two of us walk the rest of the way home on separate sides of the road, as usual. But now I feel as if there's a bigger distance between us than ever. Because if our fathers aren't really brothers, then that means we aren't cousins at all!

I don't have long to worry about it, though, because the instant I step through the back door, I know something is wrong. Maman isn't in the kitchen like she always is, ironing or stirring something on the stove or rolling out pie dough. And when I call out her name, it's Madame Coleman who steps lightly out of the hallway into the kitchen to greet me. She looks pretty in a gray dress the color of pigeon feathers, and a pearl necklace, but I can tell by the look on her face that she has something bad to tell me.

"*Où est* Maman?" I ask her in French, and I can see that she knows what I mean.

And then, to my complete surprise, she begins speaking French to me. It's not the same as our sort of French, and she struggles with some of the words, but she manages. She asks me to sit down at the table, then tells me that there's something wrong with Yvette, that they had to take my sister to the hospital because she was feverish and vomiting.

"But who?" I demand. My heart is pounding so hard now I can hear it in my ears. "Who took her? We don't have a car."

"One of the neighbors," Madame Coleman softly explains. "Your mother knocked on their door for help. It was the fire chief a few doors down. He drove your mother and Yvette to the hospital."

I know that the LeBlanc family has a car. They're the only ones on the street. Monsieur LeBlanc could afford to buy one because he has such a good job as fire chief. Maman walks to church with Madame LeBlanc, and sometimes she gives us her day-old pastries that they buy from Monsieur Nadeau. Maman has just started trading our butter ration coupons for Madame LeBlanc's sugar ration coupons because Maman needs the sugar for her baking, and she uses lard and shortening instead of butter. Madame LeBlanc likes to have butter on her toast every day. We never get butter on ours.

And then I can't help it. Two tears trickle slowly down my face.

"Is she going to die?" is the first thing I can say.

Madame Coleman's pretty face looks grim, and she struggles with a smile.

"Oh, I don't think so," she tells me in a slow voice as she chooses her words. "The doctors will take good care of her there. Your mother told me that there's some cold pork and potatoes in the cupboard out on the back porch that you can fry for your dinner. And your maman will be home as soon as she can with some news."

"Why do you know how to speak French?" I dare to ask, and now she smiles widely.

"Well, I studied it in school a long time ago, Aline," she explains. "And sometimes I read French magazines and newspapers to practice."

Then we hear the front door slam and Carolyn's voice calling "Mummy." She's home from school now. The Colemans always use our front door.

"Now, if you need anything, you know where we are. Just at the top of the stairs," Madame Coleman tells me, then pats my hand with her soft, slim one. Her hands aren't red and raw like my mother's because the Chinese man does her laundry—picks up and delivers! "And don't worry. Everything will be fine."

She swishes out of the room, but not before giving me a little hug, and leaves a nice smell like flowers behind. It must be her perfume. It reminds me of the purple lilacs I push my face into when the bush is blooming in our yard. I know about perfume, and I think maybe I've smelled it in church a few times, but I don't know anyone else who wears it. The smell lingers as I sit in the rocker by the stove, rocking and thinking, back and forth, back and forth. Thinking that this is all my fault because I haven't been good lately. I've been lying and stealing and doing too many not-nice things, and God is probably mad at me for that.

And even worse, I haven't been to confession yet to ask forgiveness. I sit there rocking and praying to Our Lord to make Yvette well again because I don't want to have to look at her all stiff and waxy in a casket in our living room. I just want her and Maman to be home safe with us again. When my brothers come home I tell them what happened, but I don't give up my chair. I just keep on rocking and praying.

When Papa finally walks through the door, bringing in a whoosh of cold air and a dusting of fresh snow on his heavy coat and hat, I run into his arms and start to sob. Then I tell him what happened, because he doesn't even know yet, and he tries his best to comfort me while my brothers watch quietly from their chairs at the table. But my father is not the person who comforts in our house. It's Maman. Papa presses a clumsy hand on my head and tells me to keep praying and that Yvette will be fine. I can tell by his dark eyes, though, that he's worried.

Then he starts frying pork and potatoes for our supper, which never happens in our house. Papa just sits at the table, always, and waits for Maman to put a plate down in front of him and pour his tea. He seems clumsy at this task too, and looks at us apologetically when some of the potatoes fall from the frying pan onto the floor as he stirs, and he picks them up and quickly puts them back. Then he touches a finger to his lips and whispers, "Don't tell Maman."

And for the first time that evening, my two brothers and I finally manage to smile.

I lie on the bed that I usually share with my sister and spend the rest of the evening reading a Delly book to distract myself. But it's not that easy because on Yvette's pillow beside me, I can see a splotch of blood. I wonder if her throat was bleeding. Is that why she had to go to the hospital? And why isn't Maman home yet? Will she be spending the night there? And the sticky red lollipop is still in my mitten, waiting for Yvette to come home.

Papa is usually in bed early, but I can hear him pacing in the kitchen. We don't have a phone, and neither do the Colemans. And I know I won't sleep until my mother gets home. It's not the same without Maman here. The house feels empty without her soothing voice and her familiar face and her comfortable ways that always make me feel safe inside. How she makes me feel better with just a smile or a gentle hand on my shoulder. How she let me eat a whole raisin pie by myself when she knew I needed it. I can't help but think that just like our bodies have souls, Maman is the soul of this house. Without her here, our house feels dead.

What about poor Jeanine Bonenfant and her family? Their maman is dead. Her soul has gone to heaven to be with Our Lord, and they have to go on living without her. I realize that I'm blinking back tears just thinking about it. Maybe Sister Madeleine is right. No wonder Jeanine is so angry all the time and doesn't care about anything. I'm not sure I would, either, if I had her very sad life. Maybe Jeanine really does need a friend. She told Sister that I'm her friend. Maybe that's her someday dream, like mine for an "English" nose. Which feels like a very silly dream right now. Maybe Georgette was right and my own nose isn't so bad after all. Poor Georgette Blondin. I miss her and wonder how she's doing in Montreal with her grandmother, mother, and brother. And without Monsieur Blondin, the drunken chicken-eater!

Maybe Maman is right. Maybe we really are a little bit rich. And right now, my biggest dream of all is to hear Maman walk through our back door. Home safe and sound. And a few moments later, when I hear that sound, my heart leaps up with joy. I hear her quick footsteps on the floor and murmured words to Papa. Then, with the kitchen light behind her, I can see her in the hallway peering into the room where my brothers and I are supposed to be asleep.

"Maman," I whisper, and in an instant she is sitting on the bed with her cool hand on my forehead. "Is Yvette going to die?"

"Oh, non, ma belle," she says. "Don't worry, Yvette will be fine soon. I just wanted the doctor to check her. She will come home tomorrow or the day after. She has an infection and needed some special medicine."

I only realize that my face is wet with tears when my mother starts wiping them away with her sweater sleeve. Then she brushes the hair off my face and gently strokes my forehead, which is the last thing I remember before my eyes flutter shut.

14

Cheese Sandwich

The next morning, Maman tells me that I have to stay at school for lunch because she has to go back to the hospital to visit with Yvette and find out when she can some home. My stomach twists because I'm still so worried about my sister. But this morning I awoke with an idea too, for trying to find a way to be nice to Jeanine Bonenfant since she thinks I'm her friend. First I check with Maman, though, to make sure that it's all right with her. But not until I tell her about what Sister Madeleine said to me at recess yesterday.

"Poor Jeanine." Maman clucks her tongue as she scoops porridge into my bowl. She pours some cream onto it from the top of the milk bottle.

I'm the lucky one who gets it because I'm the first one up and at the table, except for Papa who is already outside in the barn with the horses. The boys are being lazy this morning, probably because the house is still so cold. But I need to talk to Maman.

"That poor family," Maman continues. "And I'm sure Sister is right. That girl needs a friend right now. And she appreciates that you went to her house to pray for her mother. Maybe she really would like you to be her friend, Aline."

I take a deep breath. I'm going to ask her right now before I lose my nerve. "Do you think, Maman, I can invite Jeanine to come to our house sometime?"

This is a difficult question for Maman to answer. We don't often have visitors in our house. I have never brought friends home, except to play in our yard, never inside. And now that our beds are in the living room and dining room and we have tenants, perhaps Maman won't want anybody to come here. Her head is down, her eyebrows knitted into a frown. I can tell she must be thinking hard about this question. And when her face lights up and she nods, I know my idea was a good one.

"Of course you can invite her to come over sometime," Maman tells me. "But not until next week, when Yvette is feeling much better, okay?"

That makes me feel a little happier. Next week is the week before Christmas holidays begin. There is so much to look forward to, with Maman's special baking and the Christmas oranges, which are a juicy treat. And the beautiful music at church. And when she comes to my house, I can show Jeanine the manger scene in the corner that Bernard has finally finished setting up. And the red accordion bells strung across the room. Maman said that le père Noël won't be able to stop at our house this year, though, and that makes me feel a little sad.

That's when I remember the broken china fruit bowl. The one that nobody else has even noticed is missing from the table this Christmas. I've scarcely thought about it myself with all the terrible things that have been going on lately. I truly do miss looking at it, and I'm so sorry that it's broken. But maybe it's not so important after all.

And maybe Maman was right when she told me that.

All the way to school in the sled, I wonder how I'll be able to ask Jeanine my question. If she's even back at school today. Will she speak to me now that she's told Sister that I'm her friend? Or will she throw snowballs at me and call me names the way she always does?

"Jeanine is Jeanine," Sister told me. And maybe she'll always stay the same.

I watch the back of Papa's big hat with the earflaps as he steers the sled and calls out commands to the horses. And I can't help but wonder if what my cousin Lucille told me is true. *Why would his mother "take in" another baby? Whose baby was it? And why did it make him so angry?* I would love to ask him those questions, but I'm afraid.

And oh, those candies still hidden in the little dresser drawer in my room! And the ten cents I stole from Maman's purse! Whenever I almost let myself forget about what I did, my guardian angel reminds me that I haven't even confessed it to Father Louis yet, and that I must, before Christmas, so I can have a pure heart and soul in time for celebrating the birth of Jesus. Today, I left the red lollipop under my pillow and made the bed myself so it's nice and tidy in case Yvette finally comes home.

We're almost at the school when I realize that I haven't even hidden under the hay this morning. My mind has been too busy worrying about so many other things. And the entire time, I've been sitting upright in the sled as Papa and I glide along through the snowy streets, fat snowflakes tumbling from the sky and plastering our coats and hats.

And today, for the first time since I can remember, I realize I don't even feel ashamed.

✳

Jeanine doesn't come to school all day again. During afternoon recess, rumors fly in the schoolyard among the girls.

"Maybe Jeanine Bonenfant's family got thrown out for not paying their rent, like Georgette Blondin's family did," one girl suggests.

"Georgette's father lost his job because he's a drunk," another girl blurts out.

Poor Georgette. If she only knew what people are saying

about her family. The Blondins with all their wonderful things. The family that I thought was so rich.

Someone else says, "Maybe Jeanine is sick and she's going to die like her Maman."

Then someone else laughs and says, "What does it matter? She's a big, dumb lazy girl anyway who lives in a dirty house with a drunk for a father." And that someone is my friend Thérèse, trying to show off in front of the other girls by saying stupid things.

I grab her by the lapel of her coat and pull her face too close to mine, and the other girls standing around us in the schoolyard gasp.

"That's a mean thing to say," I tell her loudly. "You don't deserve the same name as Sainte Thérèse! And you should go to confession for saying such terrible things about Jeanine."

"But it's true," Thérèse hisses back in my face as she struggles to break free from my grip. "You were at her house with me, Aline. You know what it was like there, with everything dirty and torn and broken. And so stinky. And you're the one who told me that she stole..."

"*Tais-toi*, Beaudoin," I yell at her. "Shut up!"

Thérèse's face hardens and her jaw stiffens. "And you're no better, Sauriol, with your stinking horses and chickens in the yard..."

Before Thérèse can spit out another mean word, I trip her in the snow, and she lands hard on her back and starts to cry. I kick snow in her face, then dash toward the school doorway as tears soak my cheeks. But before I can get there, someone grabs my arm. When I spin around, Sister Madeleine is looking down at me. And I know I must be in trouble.

"What's wrong, Aline?" she asks, and when I try, between sobs, to explain to her what just happened, what mean things some of the girls were saying, she shakes her head knowingly.

"Go inside and wash your face now," she says. Then her mouth hardens into a tight line and she walks across the schoolyard toward the group of girls I just left behind.

After recess, Sister makes us sit as still as statues while she gives a lecture about kindness and about how we must remember the sort of person Jesus was and live our lives according to His example. Especially at this time of year when we're about to celebrate His birth. Which means leading a life of love, not hate. And of spreading our love among others. Then the whole class has to write out a chapter from our catechism book for the rest of the afternoon.

I can feel everyone's eyes boring into my head as they scribble away, shaking out their hands now and then to get rid of the cramps. Sister has made her point. She expects us to do better. To act differently. This, I know for certain, is a very difficult thing to do. I've said some bad things about Jeanine, but plan on trying as best I can now, and hope the other girls in my class have listened to Sister as well.

And that they won't be too mad at me for getting the whole class in trouble today.

Just to be sure, I linger after school, wiping off the blackboard for Sister until everyone else has gone home. She doesn't have much to say, just sits at her desk with her head bowed over her work. But now and then when I look over, she's watching me, and I offer her a weak smile, which she always returns. When I leave, she thanks me for helping her today.

Just around the corner from my house, it happens. I get a snowball in the back of the head again. It stings so much that I let out a shriek. Icy slush starts melting down my neck, so cold that it almost hurts. When I spin around, I see Jeanine Bonenfant grinning at me from the other side of a fence. Has she been following me, planning this attack? Just when I'm almost certain that something might be changing between us?

"Jeanine!" When I call her name, she ducks down. "Why did you do that, Jeanine?" I call out again, and she pops back up. "I thought maybe we were friends now. And why haven't you been coming to school?"

Her mouth becomes an ugly hole as she screws up her face, then spits in the snow.

"I'm not your friend," she yells back. "I'm nobody's friend!"

I'm jolted by a shudder of dread. I try to resist the temptation to run even though my guardian angel is pushing me hard. Only because Jeanine told Sister that I was her friend.

"Jeanine, would you like to come to my house some time? Maybe at Christmastime, for some cookies and a piece of pie?" I ask her, and her face becomes a dark cloud.

"Your house? Why would I ever want to come to your house, A-de-line Sau-ri-ol?" she barks at me. "Why would I ever want to do that?"

"Well, because I've been to your house, you know, and I thought that maybe…"

"Tais-toi!" she shrieks. "Shut up! I never ever want to go to your house!" Her shrill voice bounces off the walls of all the houses, echoes across the still winter afternoon.

I take a step back. But I won't give up. "But why not, Jeanine?"

Jeanine steps out from behind the fence. She's wearing her tattered too-tight coat, torn stockings and too-big boots, only one mitten, and no hat today. She walks straight toward me, and I try my best not to move even though my wobbly legs are wishing they could run.

"Because, *stupide*," she screams right into my face. "I have nothing! And you, Sauriol, you have so much. You have everything!"

Then she spins around and runs off, disappearing around the corner into the gray winter dusk. I stand there for a moment watching her run and wondering what she meant by that. I know for sure that I don't have everything. But I don't have nothing, either. And maybe there's a difference. When she's out of sight, I shuffle through the snowy street toward home, thankful that for once Jeanine didn't beat me up, even if she says she doesn't want to be my friend.

When I get there, a man is sitting on the steps of our front porch. I know who he is. A tramp, looking for some food. Maman always gives food to hungry tramps. They knock on the front door and sit and wait for her to answer and offer them a scrap of food. But today, I don't think she's answered. She must still be at the hospital with Yvette. My brothers never come home until much later these days; Bernard plays hockey with his friends, and Arthur sits and reads in the Carnegie Library. Papa isn't home yet, either.

I slip through the back gate and into my yard. There's half a cheese sandwich in my schoolbag since I was too worried about everything to finish my lunch today. And often Maman gives the tramps a small glass of milk too, which I plan on doing myself right now. But I stop and gasp when I run up to my back stoop. Carolyn is standing there, and she's crying.

"Aline, there's a scary man out front," she says. And I understand right away. When she came home from school a few minutes ago, the tramp was on the front porch, and she must have been too frightened to go inside so she ran around back.

"*Viens.* Come," I tell her, opening the back door.

"But what if there's another one inside your house?" she whispers.

"Non," I say laughing. "Viens *voir*. Come see."

I lead her into the kitchen, kick off my boots, and take the sandwich, wrapped in brown paper, out of my bag. It's a bit stiff and cold, but it's still good. I take the bottle of milk off the windowsill where it stays cool, and I pour a small glass. Then I gesture to Carolyn to follow me to the front door. Her eyes are wide, and she looks scared.

"Open de door," I tell her in my broken English, and she does.

The tramp is still sitting there. He looks up at us with hope in his eyes and offers a whiskery, toothless smile when I hand him the sandwich and the glass.

"Merci, *mademoiselle*," he murmurs. He will leave the glass there on the front porch when he finishes. They always do.

"*De rien, monsieur. A votre santé*," I say, wishing him good health before I close the door.

Carolyn is still staring, wide-eyed. "You mean that scary man was hungry?" she says, and when I nod, she smiles.

Then she runs up the steps to the top floor of our house as music drifts from the radio in the room where her mother is waiting.

Maman has left a pot of pea soup on the stove for our supper. I sit at the long table to do my homework while I wait for everyone else to come home as the light fades from the kitchen windows. And only realize that I've fallen asleep with my head on my arms when the sound of the back door jolts me awake. It's Papa, and he's beaten my brothers home tonight. He's much earlier than usual.

"Is Maman here?" he asks, looking hopeful. When I shake my head, his face sags.

Papa hangs up his winter clothes, sits in the rocker by the stove, and begins to rock. The chair creaks. It's the only sound. The radio isn't playing upstairs anymore. Papa and I are here in the kitchen alone. That never happens. And I have something important to ask him, but I don't even know where to begin. So instead I pour him a cup of tea from the teapot on the stove, then set a plate with a piece of bread and a slab of pork in front of him. He grunts his thanks.

"Papa, we haven't heard many Ti-Jean stories lately," I tell him as I pull my chair up to the table again.

Papa shakes his head as he chews. "That's true, ma fille," he says with a sigh. "I haven't been in the mood. Too tired, too worried." His voice fades away as he speaks, and he shrugs, looking sad.

"Can I tell you one?" I ask, and he looks surprised.

"Oui, Aline," he says, nodding and almost smiling. "You have a Ti-Jean story too?"

"I made one up myself, Papa," I say. "Only her name is Ti-Jeanne."

"It's about a girl?" Papa says and smirks when I nod. "Bon, let's hear it then."

And so I start my story, not really sure where I'm going with it but taking a chance just the same. It's the only way I can think of to talk about something that is never allowed.

15

Ti-Jeanne

Once there was a girl named Ti-Jeanne who lived with her family in a big fieldstone house that her papa built all by himself. She had a maman too, and a sister and two brothers."

"*Comme nous*," Papa says grinning. Like us.

I nod again. "There were horses and chickens in the backyard, and a skating rink that Papa built for his children too. He liked to call them 'little chickens,' those four children of his." When Papa smiles even wider, it gives me the courage to continue. "Ti-Jeanne knew her Papa was happy most of the time. But he didn't smile very much, and she didn't know why."

Now Papa frowns, just a little, then realizes it and tries to force a smile as he nods at me.

"He had enough food to eat every day, a warm, cozy house to live in, and a nice rocking chair by the stove that he sat in every night." Papa closes his eyes to listen as I continue.

"Across the road was another house, not as nice as Ti-Jeanne's, made of wood, not stone." Papa stops rocking. His eyes fly open and he watches me, his eyebrows a thick black line. I can feel my heart beat harder as I start talking faster and faster. "In that house lived another family, with three children of their own. But the children in those two families never spoke to one another. They didn't even look at one another because they weren't allowed, even though all the children in those two houses were cousins and their Papas were brothers."

Papa's jaw stiffens, and I look away. "Aline," he warns me, his voice like a storm.

"And the little girl who lived in that house was the best of friends with Ti-Jeanne. But their papas didn't know it because they never ever spoke to each other. They never even looked at each other. They always seemed to be mad at each other. So the two cousins could never let them find out about their friendship, all because of something that happened a long, long time ago."

Papa's hand slams the table hard, and I jump. "Adéline!" he growls. "*Arrête-toi!*"

But I don't stop talking. "Papa," I whisper. "What really happened a long time ago?" And then I actually say it. "Is…is Uncle Pierre not really your brother?"

Papa's face turns dark red, and he seems to be quaking with anger as he rises slowly to his feet. He reminds me of one of the bad giants that he tells us about in his own Ti-Jean stories. But

Papa has never ever hit me, or anyone else in our family. He would never pull trees out of the ground and throw them. He's not that kind of papa.

"I don't know where you could ever have heard such nonsense, Aline. But don't you ever, *ever* ask me that question again," he says in a quaking voice.

Then he shuffles through the hallway into the dining room, where his bed is now, and I hear the springs squeak when he lies down.

And then, just a few minutes later, the wonderful sound of boots stomping on the back porch and a blast of cold air when the door bursts open, and the boys and Maman tramp into the kitchen. I run into her arms to hug her, and she rubs her icy, red cheek against my warm one.

"Yvette? Where is she?" I ask, almost afraid to hear the answer.

"Still there, ma belle," Maman says as she shrugs off her coat. "But much better."

"It's good news," Arthur says, grinning as he warms his hands by the stove. "Yvette will be coming home tomorrow."

"We walked over to the hospital after school to wait for Maman and come home with her," Bernard adds.

"They're nice boys, your brothers," Maman adds, then suddenly looks concerned. "But where's Papa?"

"*Ici*," says a voice. "Right here, Maman." Papa stands in the kitchen doorway watching us all. And he almost seems to be smiling.

Tomorrow. Tomorrow. Yvette will be home tomorrow.

Those words soothe me to sleep like the lullabies Maman used to sing for us so long ago. Maman doesn't sing much anymore.

The next day is Saturday, and I walk over to the Carnegie Library after breakfast with Lucille. On Saturdays, we always meet around the corner at ten in the morning. to go to our favorite place in the world. I even love the way the library smells, and the shelves and shelves of books, each one of them hiding a brand-new story, mostly in English, which I can't read very well yet, but maybe someday.

The whole time that Lucille and I are in the library choosing our books, I can barely hold on to the story of what I asked Papa yesterday about *mon oncle* Pierre. It flutters like a butterfly inside me, trying to get free. Finally, I can't keep it in any longer. As we stand side by side between the bookshelves scanning all the colorful spines, I move a little closer and give Lucille a nudge.

"Guess what, Lucille," I whisper. "I asked Papa yesterday about what happened a long time ago between our fathers."

Lucille gasps. "*Vraiment*?" Really? she practically shouts.

"*Silence*, les filles." When we look over, the librarian is glaring at us from behind her desk, finger to her lips.

"Oui. I made up a little story about it. He got really mad at me," I admit to her in a quiet voice. "His face turned all red, and he was even shaking."

"Oh, Aline, you're the bravest girl I know," my wide-eyed cousin tells me. "I would never take a chance like that with my papa. Why did you do it?"

I frown for a moment. Then I smile.

"Because if we don't ask questions, then how will we ever know the truth?" I tell her.

A few hours later, I run all the way home with Lucille trying her best to keep up, and sure enough, Yvette is there. Home safe in her bed.

Papa went over to the hospital in the sled with Maman this morning. They took plenty of wool blankets and a hot-water bottle to keep Yvette warm on the ride home. I open the front door and wave my scarf in the air. That's my signal to tell the good news to Lucille, who is waiting across the street on her front porch to find out. Then I run back inside to fetch the lollipop from under my pillow.

Yvette is pale. She still can't speak outside of a whisper. She won't be able to go back to school until after Christmas. But at least she's home with us now.

"Yvette," I say. "Hold out your hand."

Her eyebrows become question marks, but she does what I ask and holds out one small hand. And that's where I put the lollipop. And that's when her eyes light up and she smiles. I haven't seen my sister smile like that for the longest time.

"Oh, Aline, merci," she whispers and puts it right into her mouth. Even though it's a little matted with wool from my mitten, she doesn't care. Then she takes it out for a moment. "But where did you get it?" she asks.

"That's a big secret," I tell her, and she smiles again. "Hide it from Maman, okay, and give me the stick when you're done."

She just nods and licks and nods and licks.

Christmas is coming fast. Yvette's throat continues to heal, and every day she can eat a little more of everything—not just custards and eggs and tapioca. Soon she can eat finely chopped meat and boiled potatoes, and she is almost back to normal again. She's still pale, though, and still not in class, but she's doing the schoolwork that I bring home for her each day.

At school, all the girls in the schoolyard talk about what they'll be receiving from le père Noël. I have very little to say about it, though, and stand at the edge of the circle of girls, thinking about other things. They didn't stay mad at me very long after I pushed Thérèse down that day and let her have it. Even she didn't stay mad and has never said another word about it, though she doesn't talk much to me anymore and I don't really care. Everyone seems to be acting a little nicer, a little kinder. Trying not to be mean to one another. Maybe because it's Christmastime.

Or maybe they really listened to Sister after all.

My mind is still full of questions that I can't answer, like what's become of Jeanine? After that day when she popped up from behind the fence, threw snow at me, and spit, I haven't seen her. After more than a week, I've given up. I guess we're really not friends after all. But I can't stop worrying about her and her family, and what a sad Christmas they're going to have. *You have everything and I have nothing*, she yelled at me the last time I saw her. And now I think I'm beginning to understand even more what she meant by that.

I'm getting used to living with tenants in the upstairs, to sneaking quickly up the steps to the bathroom like a timid mouse in my own house. Whenever I'm up there, I steal a peek into the rooms if their doors are open and admire all the Colemans' bright and shiny things that I can see on the sideboard—our sideboard—and on the dining room table, which is also ours. It looks cozy in their rooms and smells heavenly, like perfume and furniture polish, and roasting meat, and even the cigarette smoke that drifts out now and then, all so mysterious and strange. And there's the wonderful radio music too. I wish I could take a better look inside those rooms where the Coleman family lives.

Now that I don't have to worry so much about Yvette anymore, I've been thinking about the missing fruit bowl. Poor Maman. She must feel so sorry about breaking it. We're still waiting for one of the other children to ask about it, and that hasn't happened yet, so they don't even know that Maman had to throw all the pieces in the garbage.

And Papa hasn't ever mentioned my Ti-Jeanne story since I told it that day. Sometimes I catch him looking at me funny, and

I smile at him, and he raises his eyebrows. I wonder what he's thinking and if he's curious about why I asked him that question about my uncle. But I won't mention it, because I don't want his face to turn all red like a giant again!

But now I have my biggest worry to face. It's the Saturday before Christmas, and I have to go to confession once and for all, to confess to Father what I did when I stole that dime from Maman's purse. The sin has been floating above me like benediction smoke in church, and I want to be rid of it so I can free my mind again and enjoy Christmastime.

Which is why I kneel quietly in a church pew on Saturday morning, thinking about all these other things while I avoid getting into the line for confession. There's a big lineup today. I recognize so many girls from school, some of them with their parents. I suppose we all want to be sin-free for Christmas. I often wonder what sort of sins parents have to confess and why they even have to go to confession. They're grown-up, so they must know better by now. Finally, I force myself to leave the pew and get in line behind everyone else. Usually I'm very impatient about waiting in line, about waiting for anything. But today, I wish the lineup was even longer because I don't want my turn to come.

But it does. I kneel down behind the curtain in the confessional, and when Father slides open the little door, I begin my prayer and my confession. I start with all the usual sins, the easy ones that Father hears all the time, the ones that won't surprise him. I disobeyed my parents. I had a fight with my brothers. I called my sister names. I talked back. Sometimes it's hard to come up with sins. Sometimes I even make them up. Father must get tired of hearing the same sins over and over again from me. But today will be different, that's for sure.

I tell him about the half an orange that Carolyn gave me and that I didn't share. I still feel guilty about that and try to explain. But Father Louis stops me mid-sentence.

"Adéline," he says. "That orange was a present, wasn't it?"

Father knows exactly who is talking to him. He always does.

"Yes, I guess it was, Father."

"Then it's not a sin that you ate the orange yourself. Continue."

And that's when tears flood my eyes and I find it hard to speak.

"Father, I did something very bad. I stole ten cents from Maman's purse." I say it quickly, hoping, maybe, that if he didn't hear right, he won't bother asking me to repeat myself. I'm met with silence. And I'm sure now that he heard.

"But Father," my voice picks up speed. "It was for the church charity box. Maman never has any money to spare, and I felt ashamed because I couldn't help, so I took some. But only to help those poor destitute families. And I'm so sorry."

"Well, Adéline," he says, after clearing his throat. "Then you should tell your Maman what you did. You did it because you were trying to be charitable."

And now I have to tell Father the rest of my sin, the biggest part. The part I've been holding on to in my heart for so long. And when I do, the tears finally spill out and I'm almost choking on my words. I tell him about the box being gone from Sister's desk and how Lucille and I spent the money on candy. And how Lucille threw up and how I felt sick afterwards too, and brought the rest home.

"I see," Father says. "And what will you do with the rest of that candy?"

"I don't know, Father. I ate a peppermint, and I gave a peppermint to Jeanine Bonenfant when her mother died, to help her feel better. And I gave a red lollipop to my sister after she got her tonsils out, to help *her* feel better."

"Bon," Father says. "That was a nice thing for you to do, Adéline. And I'm sure you'll find something nice to do with the rest of that candy too. Maybe you should tell your mother about what you did. I think she might understand."

And that's all Father says to me. He doesn't get mad or lecture me. He just forgives me for my sins, then tells me to say my penance: a decade of the rosary, three Our Fathers, and an Act of Contrition. When I leave the confessional, I feel lighter, happier than I have for many, many days because I've finally told Father the truth about what I did.

Not only am I now free of sin, I've also decided what to do with the rest of that candy.

16

$\mathscr{F}$ruit and $\mathscr{C}$hocolate

The Wednesday before Christmas is our last day of school. All the girls are squirming in their seats. Sister is having trouble keeping our attention, and she doesn't even get mad at us. She knows that we are extra excited because Christmas is on Friday and that everyone can't stop chattering about it.

So after recess she gives up and tells us to just talk quietly in our seats or play cards, which we've been allowed to bring to school today. I sit at my desk playing Solitaire and thinking about what our Christmas will be like this year. And it doesn't make me smile as brightly as so many of the other girls in the class. I also know, by glancing around at all the faces, that I'm not the only one struggling with my feelings. Some of the other girls won't be having a visit from le père Noël, either. Some of the other girls will have empty stockings too. Then, just before the final bell rings, Sister glides over to my seat and lightly touches me on the shoulder.

"Please stay behind for a moment after the last bell," she says, and I nod.

I wonder if this is about Jeanine again. She still hasn't come back to school. Nobody is certain what's become of her, though some of the girls have seen her wandering around the neighborhood and several have taken a snowball in the head just like I did. Poor Jeanine. It's very hard to make myself feel sorry for her when she acts like that. But whenever I think about being at her house, about the sad Christmas they'll be having, it becomes much easier.

I approach Sister's desk after all the other girls have left the classroom. She's received beautiful cards and even a few presents from some of the girls, but not from me. Maman doesn't have money to buy Christmas greeting cards or gifts for our teachers. Sister opens a drawer and takes out a package wrapped in brown paper and tied with string.

"This is for you, Aline," she tells me. "Open it up when you get home, okay?"

My mouth has dropped open. "But Sister, why? I don't have a present for you."

"Oh, it's not really a present," Sister Madeleine explains. "It's to say thanks, for helping me so much and for helping Jeanine too. It's something you need. You'll understand when you open it. And I'd like to wish you and your family a joyous Christmas, Aline," she adds.

I have no words. All I can think of is to run around the desk and hug Sister, and she looks surprised for an instant before she smiles. Then I run out the door and all the way home with the package under my arm. Lucille runs along behind me calling out questions that I don't have the patience to answer. Because nobody, besides my parents, has ever given me a present before in my life. And I can't wait to get home and tear it open!

But I do wait, until suppertime, when everyone is at home and gathered around the kitchen table to watch. I'm eager myself, but a part of me wants to wait a bit longer because I don't really want the excitement to end. Even though my brothers and Yvette haven't stopped pestering me to hurry up and open that package.

I do it slowly. I untie the string instead of cutting it. Maman saves everything. Then I carefully fold back the brown paper because she'll save that too. And inside, I can't believe my eyes! There's another layer of paper, but this time it's Christmas paper, with green, white, and red bells. It's the prettiest paper I've ever seen in my whole life.

"Ohhh," Yvette whispers, wide-eyed, then reaches out a finger to touch it. "You're so lucky, Aline."

"Sister Madeleine must really like you," Arthur adds. "I wonder why." He has a teasing smile. He and Bernard start laughing and so do Maman and Papa.

"Well, open it, silly," Bernard says. "What are you waiting for?"

I'm very careful not to tear the Christmas paper. I'm keeping that for myself. As soon as I saw it, I had plans for it. I gasp when I see what's inside. A scrapbook! And tin-can labels of every sort, from pies to vegetables to soups. And there are even a couple of ladies' magazines full of colorful pictures. I've never had a magazine before.

"You are so very, very lucky," Yvette murmurs. And when I look at her, I realize that her eyes have filled with tears. I hand her one of the magazines, and she gasps.

"We can share them, Yvette. I have to cut out pictures of food and put them into this scrapbook for a school project. You can help me, okay?"

Yvette grabs my arm and hugs it. I think she's happy! I know I am. Maman and Papa are smiling too, and I think I see tears in Maman's eyes as she serves our supper of roast pork, potatoes, and cabbage—but I'm not sure why she would cry.

For the rest of the evening, Yvette and I cuddle up on our bed and pore over one of the magazines, studying each page carefully, absorbing all the lovely pictures of mothers in their nice kitchens, of children playing, of fathers smoking their pipes and reading the paper. And making sure that we have plenty left to look at tomorrow before we finally turn out our lamp.

Today is Christmas Eve, and this afternoon Maman is very busy in the kitchen, just like she's been all week. She's still baking cookies and apple pies and raisin buns and *tourtières*, the delicious meat pies that we always eat on Christmas after Midnight Mass. The boys have gone out somewhere, Papa isn't home from delivering wood yet, and Yvette has fallen asleep on the bed with her magazine spread open on her lap to a page that she just can't tear her eyes from. It's an advertisement for Whitman's chocolates, and there are boxes and boxes of them, all looking so dark and delicious and tempting, some even wrapped in shiny foil. Before she fell asleep, my sister told me that she wished she could reach right into that picture and take out a chocolate from one of those candy boxes, just one, and she'd be so very happy.

I'm sitting by the stove in Papa's rocker, reading, as Christmas music floats down the stairway from the Colemans' rooms. It's a wonderful sound, and for the first time I feel lucky that they're living up there and we get to share their music down here. I catch Maman humming along to a Christmas carol, and I smile. But there's still no fruit bowl on the table, and still nobody has asked about it. With everything else that's been happening, it's no wonder.

Maman and I hear a sudden thumping on the front porch and a loud knock. Maman looks surprised.

"Go and answer," she tells me, holding up her flour-coated hands.

I run down the hall. When I throw open the front door, a blast of icy air and snowflakes comes swirling inside. And the only thing standing there is a bushy Christmas tree. The branches rustle mysteriously, then Mr. Coleman pokes his head around the side with a toothy grin. There's snow sprinkled like sugar on his hat and on his shoulders.

"Hello, Aline," he says. "Would you please call my daughter down here to help me carry this tree upstairs?"

A Christmas tree in our house! We've never had one before today. I can smell the woodsy fragrance of pine and can't stop myself from touching one of the prickly green branches. "I can 'elp you, Monsieur Coleman," I tell him.

"Oh, would you, love?" Monsieur Coleman says. "Let me just stamp the snow off my galoshes, and I'll be right with you."

Maman is standing in the hallway watching, her floury hands still in the air.

"Don't stay up there too long," she warns me. "And don't be a bother, okay, Aline?"

"I won't, Maman, I promise," I tell my mother as Carolyn's father steps inside. He tips the tree over and lifts up the trunk, and I take hold of the top bough, the part that the angel or the star will sit on. At least, that's what I've seen in pictures and in other people's houses, but it has never ever happened in ours. Monsieur Coleman walks up the steps carrying his end, and I walk behind him carrying mine. We drop the tree in the hallway, and Monsieur Coleman begins nailing two slats to the trunk.

I stand quietly and peer into one of their rooms, the room where they will put their Christmas tree and where there is a sofa and some chairs and a table for eating on—the one that matches the buffet that's downstairs in the old dining room where Maman and Papa sleep now. The room that once was mine and Yvette's! Carolyn is sitting in a maroon armchair, holding one of her dolls. She waves at me, and I wave back. She's wearing a beautiful red velvet dress, and so is her doll. The exact same one. I can't believe it!

"*Joyeux Noël*, Aline," Madame Coleman says to me with a smile as she steps out of the bedroom that has become their kitchen. She has on a green wool dress and pearls. "How is your sister doing? I hope she's feeling much better now," she tells me in her slow French.

Carolyn, still sitting in the armchair, begins to giggle.

"Yes, much better," I tell her, feeling shy, standing there in a room in my own house that feels completely strange to me now.

"I'm so glad to hear that," she says again in French.

"You're talking funny, Mummy," Carolyn tells her.

"I'm speaking French, darling," she tells her daughter. "And you will someday too, you'll see. Why don't you come in and sit down for a few minutes," she tells me, this time in English, but I know what she means.

And I do, right on the edge of their sofa that used to be in our living room, which is now our bedroom. I can't help but gaze in wonder at all the pretty things decorating this room now. There's a white lace cloth on the table that has been set for three at one end, with beautiful flowered plates and shining, silvery knives and forks. At the other end are some bottles with amber liquid in them and bright glasses with long stems that look like crystal tulips. In the center, there's a bowl with a mountain of bananas and oranges, pears and grapes. I've never seen so much fruit in one place.

My eyes land on a stack of presents in the corner, all wrapped up with beautiful paper, like what Sister wrapped my scrapbook with.

"Those are for under the Christmas tree," Carolyn tells me. I understand immediately. "From my aunties and grandmother in England."

"Would you like to help us decorate the tree?" Madame Coleman asks, smiling.

I can't believe what I've just heard, but I shake my head. I know it wouldn't be fair to Yvette or my brothers, to do something as splendid as that without sharing it with them. Monsieur Coleman has set the tree in the corner, where an open cardboard box awaits. I can see shining balls in silver, gold, red, green, and blue, each nestled in a little square space, all waiting to be hung from the tree. And a sparkling silver star too.

I can't stop myself from looking everywhere in this room. I hope I'm not being a bother, like Maman warned me. On some wall shelves, there are statues of ladies in fancy dresses, and of horses and dogs. A dessert plate on the coffee table is piled high with dark, cherry-mottled fruitcake and the whitest shortbread I've ever seen in my life. In another glass bowl, there's a heap of shiny chocolates in all different shapes, some wrapped in gold, like in the picture in the magazine. As I stare at them, I realize my mouth is watering.

"Go ahead and eat some," Madame Coleman tells me in French. "We have plenty."

Do I dare? Yes, I do. I've been invited after all, and I can't resist. I take a plump one shaped like a tiny tuque. It bursts when I bite into it. Sweet pink cream drips out, and I catch it with my tongue. And there's a cherry inside. It's the best thing I've ever tasted in my life.

"Can I take one for my sister?" I ask. "One of these?" I point to one of the foil-wrapped chocolates, and Carolyn's mother smiles.

"Bien sûr," she tells me. "Take a few. We have too many, anyway. And would you like to take some fruit, as well? Carolyn told me that you love oranges. Help yourself. Take whatever you'd like, Aline."

"Oh, no, I shouldn't," I tell her. "Maman will get mad."

"No, she won't," Madame Coleman says. "It's Christmas, after all. It's a gift. And we're living in your lovely house. We're happy living here, you know. Do take some."

I smile. Bananas! I've never even tasted one. Maybe just one banana and one orange. They're so perfect they don't even look real.

"Merci," I tell them. I stand up and reach across the table for the fruit.

And then I gasp. Their fruit bowl is bone china, with red and green holly and berries, and a thin gold line painted around the rim.

17

So Many Secrets

I can't speak. I stand there staring at the bowl and find myself blinking tears from my eyes.

"What's the matter?" Carolyn's mother asks, looking concerned. "Is something wrong, Aline?"

"It's nothing," I whisper, then touch the rim of the bowl. *We used to have a bowl just like this one*, I'm thinking. *But Maman broke it in too many pieces to fix.*

"Isn't that a pretty bowl?" Carolyn says brightly. "Mummy bought it from Mister Nadeau, the bread man, just last week. He thought we'd like it because it's made in England."

I almost understand the words that are coming out of Carolyn's mouth. But I'm not sure I understand exactly what they mean. Or maybe I just don't want to.

"I have to go now," I tell them, then turn and run from the

room into the hallway and down the stairs, into the warm kitchen where Maman is finishing up her baking.

The kitchen smells wonderful. The steaming golden pies cooling on the counter look perfect, just like Maman's pies always do. So do the shiny brown buns speckled with raisins.

"That was fast," Maman says, smiling. "I think I'll give one of my tourtières to the Colemans. Maybe you can take it upstairs when it cools off a little. And some raisin buns too."

I sit down at the table and stare at my mother.

"Quoi?" she says, frowning, then wipes her hands on her apron and sits across from me.

"Carolyn's mother has a fruit bowl just like ours. *Is* it ours, Maman?"

When Maman bows her head, I have my answer.

"Why did you lie to me? And why did you give the bowl to Monsieur Nadeau?" I ask her, too angry to cry. "He sold it to them, you know, to the Colemans. Why, Maman?"

Maman raises her head slowly. Her face is stiff, her eyes narrow.

"Because he said he liked it. And I needed the extra money, Aline," she tells me in a quiet voice. "To help out with our Christmas, and with the doctor visits before Yvette's operation. I never thought he'd be selling it back to our tenants, though."

I swallow hard. The truth is worse than I thought. And it's all because of me, and the ten cents I stole, and that candy, which

I've secretly wrapped up in the pretty paper from Sister. In five small packages. My plan is to put one into each of our stockings tonight—my brothers', my sister's, and my own—when everyone has gone to sleep. And the fifth, I will deliver to Jeanine's house before Midnight Mass tonight.

But it's my fault that the china fruit bowl is on the Colemans' table now instead of ours. I was thoughtless and stole money from Maman's purse, so now we don't have enough money for our own family for Christmastime.

That's when my tears finally come, with deep gulping sobs, as I bury my face in my arms.

"Aline," Maman gasps. "It's only a bowl, and nobody else in the family has even noticed that it's missing. Why are you crying, ma belle?"

Now it's time for my real confession. And that's when it all spills out: what I did that day in the kitchen when I climbed up on the counter and took ten cents; and how the charity box was already gone; and how Lucille and I ate candy, and Lucille threw up on her boots; and how I hid the rest in the little dresser and gave a peppermint to Jeanine and a red lollipop to Yvette. The entire time, I'm waiting for Maman to get mad at me. But instead of yelling, she smiles wider and wider as my story pours out. And then she stands up, walks around the table, and hugs me! Which makes me howl even harder as I bury my face in her arms.

"Aline, Aline. Hush now. I didn't even notice the ten cents missing from my purse. We needed more than just one dime, ma belle. I even sold some of my pies and buns to Monsieur Nadeau to sell to others. And it was a secret, until just now. Hush, don't cry."

"But why did Monsieur Nadeau do that?" I mumble into Maman's apron, and she sighs.

"I don't know, Aline. Maybe he needed the money too. Who can say? I really should find the time to bake my own bread so that he doesn't have to come to our back door at all anymore. But where is the rest of that candy? Did you already eat it all?"

"Oh, no, Maman. That would be too greedy," I tell her.

"Did you throw it away?" she asks.

"I almost did. But that would be wasting, wouldn't it, Maman?" I say.

"Yes, Aline, it would be. Well then, what did you do with the rest of the candy?" she says, looking down at me with her eyebrows asking questions.

I offer her a slow smile as I brush my tears away. "It's a secret," I tell her.

"A secret?" My mother looks even more surprised now.

"That's right, but you'll find out what it is very soon." I smile mysteriously at her, and she smiles back at me, then gently touches my cheek.

"So many secrets," Maman says, shaking her head. "Do you have any more surprises for me today?"

When I nod, her eyes open wide. Then I take a deep breath before sharing this one, the biggest secret I know.

"Papa and Uncle Pierre aren't really brothers," I tell her and wait for her reaction.

She sits down hard on a chair and scrubs her face with her hands. Then she stares at me.

"Who told you that?"

"That's a secret too, Maman."

"It was Lucille, wasn't it?" Maman says. "I see you walking with her sometimes, you know. And talking to her. I know that you're good friends, and that's okay."

"I asked Papa, one day when you were at the hospital with Yvette," I finally admit.

"You did, Aline?" Maman gasps. "What a curious girl you are!"

"And he got mad at me and said to never ask him again. Why, Maman? Why aren't they brothers? Who is Uncle Pierre really?"

Maman sighs and shakes her head. She places both her hands on the table and looks me right in the eye.

"They are cousins, Aline, Papa and your Uncle Pierre. Their mothers were sisters. Pierre's real mother couldn't look after her baby because she didn't have a husband, so she gave the baby to Papa's mother and father to care for, to your grandparents, who died before you were even born."

"You mean they were cousins, Papa and mon oncle, just like me and Lucille?" I ask, and Maman nods. "But I would like it if Lucille had to be my sister. I wouldn't get mad like Papa did. Why did he get mad about that?"

"That might be hard to explain," Maman says in a quiet voice. "I'm not even sure Papa understands himself anymore. Times were hard then. They had a lot of children to feed in that house. Papa was one of the oldest and had to leave school and go out to work at an early age. Maybe it made him angry that they took in another child when they already had fourteen children of their own. Yes, it was a long time ago, but I suppose he's just too stubborn to fix things now."

"Are Lucille and I still cousins, though?" I ask, and Maman nods again.

"Yes, of course. You're still related because your fathers are related. You're second cousins with all the children in that family. Do you understand a little better now?" Maman reaches across the table and strokes my hand.

"Oui, Maman," I tell her, even though I really don't.

Some things in this world are just too hard to ever understand.

Later that evening, our whole family sits in the kitchen waiting until it's time to leave and walk over to church just before midnight for Mass. We're all wearing our most "decent" clothes for such a special occasion. The checkerboard is on the table, as well as some cards. Papa has taught us all to play euchre, which we're doing now to pass the time. He's already told us a Ti-Jean Christmas story, and I caught him looking at me in a strange way as he was telling it and making us laugh. I think maybe he remembers my Ti-Jeanne story.

I can hear my stomach grumbling. We didn't have a big supper, just a light snack, because we have to fast a little. When we get home after Midnight Mass, though, then we will feast—on the tourtières and the other delicious things that Maman has made for tonight and tomorrow. Earlier, Yvette, Bernard, and I tried our best to lie down quietly for a nap, but we were too excited and teased one another, instead.

When we hear thumping footsteps on the front porch and a sharp rap on the door, everyone looks surprised.

"I'll get it," Maman says, telling Papa to sit down because he's still tired from working.

I run along behind, because I'm curious too. And when Maman answers the door, there's a man standing there in a heavy overcoat and fedora, with a big smile on his raw, red face.

"Society of Saint Vincent de Paul," he says. "I have a package for the Sauriol family."

Maman's face drops, and I know why. It's a Catholic charity for the poor. I know what's in those boxes. Food and clothing for poor families in the Saint-François parish. Sister told us all about it when she explained the charity box on her desk. To collect money for the poor. It must mean we're really poor if they're delivering a charity box to our house. I don't care, though. It's another present for our family. And then from behind us, one word.

"Non." We both spin around. Papa is standing there, his face a hard mask. "No charity for this family," he murmurs and turns back toward the kitchen.

"But Papa," I say, running after him. "If we can give something to help others, like Maman gives scraps of food to the tramps whenever they knock on the door, then why can't someone else give something to help us?"

"Oh, Papa," Yvette half sobs. "Can't we have it? Please?"

Beside her, Bernard nods, his dark eyes wide and pleading. Arthur sits at the table with his legs crossed, looking solemn as usual.

"Your Papa is right, les enfants," Maman says behind me, and when I turn around she has a strange look on her face. "Other people need that box more than we do this year. You all know that, don't you?"

I do know that. Now. We really do have plenty for the six of us to share this Christmas. "*C'est vrai*, Maman," I tell her. It's true. "Papa, it's okay. I'll tell the man that we don't need it. I'll tell him to give the box to somebody else."

Papa smiles and nods at me. My younger brother and sister look disappointed, and I can tell that Arthur doesn't care. The man is still standing at the front door, smiling, but his face drops when I tell him that we won't be taking the box after all, that he should give it to another family. Maman stands behind me with her hand on my shoulder. She squeezes gently.

"That's very kind of you," he says. "Joyeux Noël to you and your family." Then he walks off into the frozen night air.

As Maman shuts the door and steers me back to the kitchen with her hand still on my shoulder, I glance toward the top of the stairs. Madame Coleman is standing by the banister watching us. She smiles at me when she sees me looking up at her.

Even Yvette is coming along to church tonight, and she is so excited, wiggling on a kitchen chair shortly before we have to leave for Mass. She's wearing her brown velvet dress that used to be mine, that probably once even belonged to somebody else before me. She's also excited because le père Noël will come during the night while we're sleeping. Maman hasn't told her that he won't be coming this year. I hate to think about how disappointed she'll be, which is why I have my own surprise for everyone.

As well as for the Bonenfant family, which I will drop off before church. I'll knock on the door and run away. I've already told Maman that part of my secret because I couldn't hold on to it anymore, and she said she'd walk over with me, then we'd meet the rest of our family in church. I don't care if Jeanine hates me. I'm still leaving some of the candy for her family, wrapped in the pretty paper with the red, white, and green Christmas bells from Sister Madeleine.

And still, nobody has asked about the missing china fruit

bowl that's sitting in the middle of the Colemans' table upstairs right now instead of on ours down here.

Then Maman hands me one of her tourtières.

"Take this upstairs to the Colemans," she tells me, then sets some raisin buns on top. "They won't go to church until morning. When you come back down, you and I will walk over to Mechanicsville, then meet Papa and the others in church."

"Why?" Papa says, watching the two of us closely as if he's trying to read our thoughts. "Where are you going?"

"Aline has a special delivery to make." When she smiles secretively, Papa just shrugs.

Along with the wonderful smell of roasting meat, music is floating down the stairs, and tonight it's extra special because it's all Christmas music—some carols I'm familiar with and some that are new to me. We've become so used to it now, this music playing from the radio upstairs all the time, that it doesn't even feel like a treat anymore. It's not so bad after all, having Protestants living in our house. Except for that fruit bowl. I won't even glance at it, I decide. I'll just hand them the baked goods quickly and leave.

I try my best not to think about the bowl as I carry the pie and buns up the steps. The doors are open to all their rooms, and they're all sitting there, in their "living room"; Carolyn's parents on the sofa and Carolyn with her beautiful doll on her lap in the maroon chair. In a corner, the decorated tree is lit up now and looks like something from a dream, shimmering with bright tinsel that reflects all the colors from the lights and ornaments and silver star. Candles are lit on the table in holders that sparkle like ice. I look away quickly so I won't have to see what else is on the table. Monsieur Coleman is smoking a cigarette. Madame is sitting primly with her hands folded on her lap. Nobody is speaking. Christmas music fills the room.

"Joyeux Noël," I say, and they all look over at once. And smile. All of them.

"Oh, Aline, won't you stay a while?" Carolyn asks, running over to me.

"I can't. We're going to Mass in a little while," I tell her. "Maman made a pie for you. And some buns."

Madame Coleman swishes over, reaches for the pie and buns, and places them on the table. Then she reaches for me and gives me a quick hug. She smells like perfume again, and I soak up the lovely scent. Monsieur Coleman comes over and solemnly shakes my hand.

"Thanks so much, my love," Madame Coleman says, this time in English. "Maybe tomorrow afternoon we can all get together, our family and yours, for a Christmas tea up here, or some such thing. All of our family is back home in England, you know."

"I'll tell Maman," I say, before hurrying back downstairs to my family.

18

Bright Shining Moments

"The Colemans want us to go up and have tea with them
tomorrow, Maman," I tell her, breathlessly. "Can we? Can
we, please? I want the others to see their beautiful tree too!"

"Bien sûr," Maman says. "That could be nice. They have no
family here in Ottawa. And I have plenty of cookies and pies left
to share. Oui, Aline, we should go upstairs tomorrow and have a
cup of tea with them."

Yvette starts jumping up and down and clapping. I know she's
desperate to play with Carolyn's lovely dolls. Papa is standing
there with another tourtière in his hand, but I'm not sure why.
And he seems to be having trouble speaking, but he's still almost
smiling. Then he steps forward, looking uncomfortable, and
hands me the meat pie. I inhale its spicy aroma.

"Aline," he says. "Put on your coat and boots and take this

across the road to your cousins' house, please. And tell them Joyeux Noël. From all of us."

I can't believe what he's just asked me to do. And I can't get my coat and boots on fast enough to do it. First I put my arm in the wrong sleeve. Then I stumble and fall on my bottom as I struggle with one of the boots, and everyone laughs.

"Good thing you weren't holding the tourtière just now," Arthur says with a grin. "And don't eat it on the way over there, either. We can all hear your stomach grumbling, you know! I'm sure that the Colemans can too, even from upstairs!"

Everyone laughs again, and so do I. That silly brother of mine!

I stomp across the snowy street, smiling up at the night sky that's bright with stars and a wide-faced moon that seems to be smiling back at me. Papa feels good about doing this. I could tell when he patted my shoulder as I was leaving just now and gently smoothed my hair. I feel good about doing it too, inside my heart, which feels as big and bright as the moon right now. When I knock on the front door a minute later, Lucille swings it open. And shrieks!

"Aline!" she says, grinning and hugging me hard as she pulls me inside.

"Watch out for the tourtière," I warn her, laughing as I hold it safely in the air.

Her brothers are standing behind her, trying to take a peek at me. And then her parents appear in the hallway behind them all, looking surprised.

"Mon Dieu!" I hear *ma tante* murmur as she puts her hand against her throat.

"Joyeux Noël from our family," I tell them and hold out our present. And smile at them.

"Mon Dieu," mon oncle says this time, to ma tante.

Lucille takes the meat pie from me. I stand there awkwardly for a moment, looking down at my boots, wondering what to do, and afraid of what Uncle Pierre and Aunt Claudine might say next. I'm not sure if they're happy or mad, and I don't want to stay there long enough to find out. So I offer them a quick wave and dash back home, where Maman is already waiting for me at the back door with her tweed coat and good hat on, and her purse hooked over her arm.

I'm not sure if anyone is home in the Bonenfant house. Nothing has changed since I was here when Jeanine's mother died, either. The front porch is still cluttered with junk. The house looks like an empty box, as sad on the outside as it is on the inside. There is only one dim lamp turned on in the front room, the room where the casket was.

Maman waits for me at the road. I turn to look at her, and she lifts her hand. Then I walk up the steps and knock, three hard raps, hoping someone will hear. There isn't a sound coming from inside, no footsteps or voices. But when I glance toward the front window, I'm sure that I see the curtains move. I leave the package of candy on the doorstep and hurry back to Maman. We link arms and start to walk toward the church, snow squeaking under our boots as Christmas bells ring out across the cold, clear night.

Behind us, I hear a door open, then close again. When I turn around, I can see a face in the window—Jeanine's—and her hand against the glass is almost waving.

The organ thunders out "Angels We Have Heard on High," and everyone at Midnight Mass sings along. Then the parishioners stream through the heavy wooden doors of Église Saint-François d'Assise, out onto the steps and streets, where everyone calls out cheerful Christmas greetings to their neighbors and friends.

My family and I are among them. All through Mass, I did my best to pay attention, but Lucille's family was sitting across the aisle. I kept leaning over to peek at her and wave, and she waved back. Maman had to nudge me three times with her elbow, but she smiled every time. I remembered to say some prayers too, especially for Jeanine Bonenfant and her family, and for Georgette Blondin and hers. Two girls I know well and who I'm sure aren't having as happy a Christmas as I am.

Lucille and her family have left the church ahead of us, but my cousin keeps turning around to wave at me. Then, at the bottom of the steps, they all stop and wait. And when our family catches up with theirs, a miracle happens! Uncle Pierre walks over to shake Papa's hand! And then Aunt Claudine reaches out and offers Maman a little hug. And they all say a few quick words to one another; I'm not sure what, but they're all smiling afterward.

And then our family sets off for Hinchey Avenue, for home.

The six of us link arms on the street, Maman and Papa on either end. Maman begins to sing in a soft voice "Il est né le divin enfant", her favorite Christmas carol. And then I hear it—a deep rumbling from Papa's chest. He's humming along with Maman in that out-of-tune way of his that means he's in a good mood. Overhead is that bright silver moon and a sprinkle of shining stars. I can't help but think that this is a bright shining moment for our family, walking home together after Midnight Mass. And I can't help but hope that many more of them will follow us home tonight. It might even be my someday Christmas dream.

When we reach home, I gaze up at Carolyn's windows. The lights are out. They're all asleep. And our own night is just beginning.

I'm the first one through the back door. I can almost taste those tourtières, which Maman had left on top of the wood-burning stove to warm up. But just inside the back door, I freeze, then let out a little yelp of surprise. Yvette pushes in behind me, and she shrieks too, then runs across the kitchen floor in her wet boots to kneel on a chair and stare at what's in the middle of the table. The rest of the family crowds in behind us, and everyone begins talking at once.

Our Christmas fruit bowl! It's heaped with oranges, bananas, grapes, and pears. And tucked among all the fruit are shining chocolates, some of them wrapped in gold.

Before even asking, Yvette reaches for the closest one and pops it into her mouth.

It's past three a.m. before our *réveillon*, our family Christmas party, has ended. We're all stuffed with the good things that Maman has been preparing over the past week as well as with fruit and chocolate from the Colemans. Tonight, the first banana I ever ate was utterly delicious. My stomach isn't grumbling anymore, either. And we've saved plenty for tomorrow. Then Maman tells us that we'd all better hurry and get to bed before le père Noël shows up and catches us still awake. And she warns us not to forget to hang our stockings on our bedposts.

Bernard and Yvette start jumping and chattering, and Maman tells them "*calmez-vous*" or they'll awaken the tenants. Then they disappear down the hallway, followed by Arthur, who walks more slowly, pretending that he's too old to care anymore. Papa is down in the cellar, adding more wood to the furnace so that the house will be warm for the Colemans, who will probably awaken before us. I'm alone with Maman in the kitchen, so I ask her.

"Le père Noël is really coming tonight?" I ask.

She looks at me with a sly smile. "It's a secret, Aline," she tells me. "You'll have to wait until morning to find out."

"But Maman, you told me…"

Maman squeezes my shoulders. "Remember how I told you I sold some pies and buns?"

I nod, understanding now. "And the fruit bowl too. But we have it back now!"

"Because of you, I'm sure, ma belle," Maman tells me. "Only because of you!"

I tell myself to keep my eyes open until Maman and Papa have fallen asleep. There's still one more thing that I have left to do tonight. But it's hard because it's so late and I'm so very tired. But I'm happy too, so happy that I'm practically hugging myself. Because after all the not-so-happy things that have been happening lately, this Christmas has been bursting with moments that I won't soon forget.

I can't help but wonder about the Dionne quintuplets. How are they spending their Christmas Eve? Did they have a réveillon like we did? I know they didn't get a Saint Vincent box stuffed with good things for their family. Are they allowed to spend Christmas with their family, or do they have to stay at the special house that was built just for them? Yes, some people think that they're such lucky girls, with all their wonderful things, their teacher, maids, and housekeepers, their lovely dresses and bounty of toys, and a grand choice of food all the time, I suppose. But they have to live behind a barbwire fence. Without any friends. So tonight, I know I'm luckier. Maybe even luckier than the two princesses who live in a palace in England.

All too soon, I lose my fight to stay awake. The next time I open my eyes, the room is filled with the dim gray light of dawn. Everyone is still snoring, though. I can hear them. I take my four little packages and place one in each stocking that hangs from the bedposts. And I'm shocked to discover that they're already bulging with gifts from le père Noël. Maman was right. He really did come last night. There's even an orange in the toe of every stocking. And now I'm adding one more present for each of us.

At last, all that candy is finally gone from my hiding spot inside the little dresser. I snuggle up under the quilt beside Yvette and fall right back to sleep with a happy heart.

The next time I open my eyes, the room is morning-bright. Maman clatters in the kitchen while Papa and the boys talk away. And on the bed beside me, Yvette has started to empty her stocking. Already, her mouth is stuffed with candies, and her face is one wide smile.

Later in the day, we're all outside skating on the rink in the yard. It's something that we've always done on Christmas day in our family, as far back as I can remember. But this time someone else is with us—Carolyn Coleman! And she's wearing her first pair of skates ever, left last night by le père Noël, who is called Saint Nicholas in England. They're dainty white ones, girls' skates, not boys' skates like ours, and they have little picks on the blades that keep making her fall down. She cried only the first time, then started to laugh when the rest of us did.

Carolyn's face is rosy with the cold. She wears stockings and her pretty plaid coat because that's all she has. Yvette and I are bundled up in our brothers' too-small breeches and coats. Nothing is ever wasted in our family! After, we will go upstairs for tea and cookies with our parents and the Colemans.

Arthur gives Carolyn a hockey stick, and that seems to help her stay on her feet. My sister and brothers and I start to shoot a horse ball around on the ice, and Carolyn won't stop laughing because she can't believe what we use for a hockey puck. A few minutes later, the backyard gate opens. It's Lucille and her brothers, who have crossed the road in their skates. From the corner of my eye, I catch a glimpse of a face in the kitchen window.

It's Papa looking out, watching us.

FIN

About

Deb Loughead is the author of more than 40 books for children and young adults, ranging from poetry and plays to picture books and novels, many of them in translation. Her Creative Non-Fiction essay, 'The Dirty Blonde in the Yellow Pajamas' appeared in Untying the Apron: Daughters Remember Mothers of the 1950s.

Deb's poetry and adult fiction have appeared in a variety of Canadian publications. (Her biggest thrill came when one of her award-winning short stories was compared to the writing style of Margaret Lawrence.) Deb has conducted writing workshops and held readings for children and adults at schools, festivals and conferences across the country.

Deb is also the author of the popular children's poetry book, All I Need and Other Poems for Kids, and the co-editor of a collection of YA body image stories entitled Cleavage: Breakaway Fiction for Real Girls, (Sumach Press, 2008). She lives with her husband Dan in Toronto. Her three adult sons have long flown the coop. For more information visit www.debloughead.ca